Stranger Session

Lauren Biel

Library of Congress Cataloging-in-Publication Data

Stranger Session/Lauren Biel 1st ed.

Cover Design: Laura at Spellbinding Design

Editing: Sugar Free Editing

Interior Design: Sugar Free Editing

For more information on this book and the author, visit: www.LaurenBiel.com

Please visit LaurenBiel.com for a full list of content warnings.

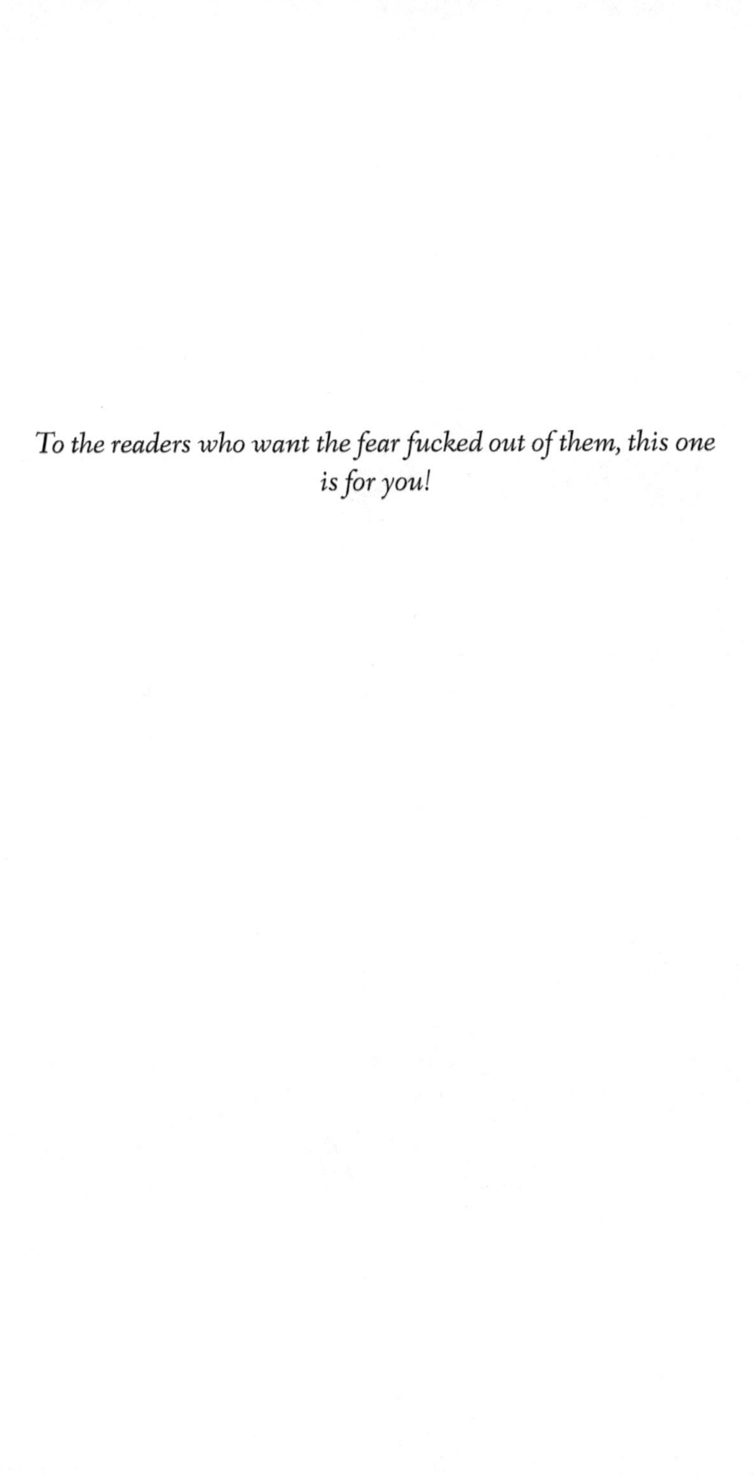

To the readers who want the fear fucked out of them, this one is for you!

Chapter One

Del

Good morning is an absolute shit way to greet the day, and I wish I could pummel the asshole who coined the phrase. There is nothing good about mornings, the time of day when we're forced to leave sleep's comforting hold. I'd stay unconscious for the next six months if I could. At least then I won't be forced to think about *her*.

The breakup was for the best, but that didn't make it any easier when it happened. Especially not the way it happened. As I warm a bowl of oatmeal and carry it to the table, I try not to think about it, but I've tried not thinking about it for months, and it hasn't worked yet.

My roommate sits across from me at the table. He shoves his bagel into his mouth and sends the little black cumin seeds all over the table. They look like roach droppings.

"We've gotta get you out of this funk," he says through a mouthful of bread. "I'm signing you up for a stranger session."

"I don't even know what that is, but my answer is still *the fuck you are.*"

Taylor rolls his eyes. "It's a blind-date photo shoot, and I don't see why you won't try it. You won't go on dates or come to any of the parties I invite you to. I feel like drastic actions need to be taken or you're going to die alone."

"I would rather be drawn and quartered." I rub a hand through my dark blond hair because I know what's coming. More guilt about my breakup.

My appetite shrivels, and I push my bowl of oatmeal away and drop my head into my hands. I don't know why he can't leave well enough alone. Yeah, I'm wallowing a bit, but I'm not eager to run out and snag another girlfriend after my last breakup. I need time to get over that. It doesn't help that I've become pretty jaded about it. I mean, I'm twenty-five and still live with a roommate.

I'd been looking for an apartment for me and my ex. When I found the perfect place, I stopped by to surprise her. She had a surprise for me too. I found her beneath one of my now ex-friends, and I ended things. Too bad I didn't know about what a lying bitch she was before I got my dick pierced for her. Maybe the next woman will appreciate it, but I have no intention of meeting her anytime soon.

My life is a depressing mess, and I don't think a weird blind date will change my six months of wallowing. Deservedly so. I fucking loved her. Or so I thought. Now I don't know what the word means.

Taylor turns his phone toward me. "Look at these girls. They're hot as fuck. They even take time to match you with the right pretty face for your personality."

I push the phone toward him. "Leave it alone, Taylor. Please."

I'm begging him to let it go. I can't deal with that. First

off, it sounds nothing like anything I would do. Ever. Second, I'm not ready, no matter how hot the girls are.

"Suit yourself. If you die alone, don't say I didn't try." He turns the screen toward himself and starts scrolling, an annoyed tightness in his lips.

I appreciate that he tries. He still invites me to things even though he knows I'll say no. "Thanks for trying, Taylor," I say. "I mean it."

"Yeah, yeah." He lifts his bagel to his mouth and sends another round of cumin-seed confetti to the table.

I dump my uneaten oatmeal into the trash, fill up my water bottle, and grab my headphones. I've gained ten break-up pounds since Lisa and I split, and I'm struggling to lose them. Even though I hate running, it passes the time and keeps my head clear. It's hard to think about my ex and how she's ruined my life when I'm struggling for my next breath. If I can lose these ten pounds, I might even agree to go on whatever blind-date activity Taylor comes up with.

But probably not.

I turn on some music and let my feet pound the pavement. Our rented house sits in a nice little subdivision filled with families and older couples. I pass lawns littered with bikes and toys, perfectly manicured grass, and well-kept garden beds. There aren't many people out and about this early, but the few I pass don't offer a wave or even a curt nod with a pinched smile. I don't quite fit in here, and they all seem to know it.

None of that mattered when I had Lisa. I fit in with someone, and that was enough for me. Now I'm a piece of driftwood floating in the open sea, unattached and alone. While I'm not in a rush to be picked up, it would be nice to be seen. Noticed.

Instead, I'm invisible.

Another runner passes on the opposite side of the street. Her blonde ponytail swishes back and forth, and her large breasts bounce despite the best efforts of the sports bra smooshing them down. Her eyes meet mine, and I expect a look of disgust because I've been caught staring, but she only smiles. The look in her eyes tells me she wouldn't mind running into me one morning.

This should excite me, but it doesn't. People are more than their outer packaging, and I want my next connection to come with an organic spark. I never had that with Lisa. She was a knockout, and that's why I wanted to be with her, but there was no substance behind her gold foil. We connected on a physical level. The sex was good, and she was nice to look at. But I see now that what we had was only skin deep.

I feel no spark with this woman either, so I keep running.

Maybe Taylor is right. Maybe I need to put myself out there more. I refuse to do that stupid photo session, but it wouldn't hurt to try dating again. If I'm being honest with myself, I don't want to be a bachelor forever. I just need to find the right woman this time. Someone who lights a fire inside me. Someone I can't stop thinking about.

Then I remember my short stint with dating apps, and a shudder runs through me. One girl ghosted me because she wrote novels for every message and I couldn't do the same. Another girl catfished me by using her sister's picture for her profile. That isn't how I want to meet someone.

I stop running, turn around, and begin jogging home. If nothing else, maybe that photo shoot would be good for a laugh. There's only one way to find out.

Chapter Two

Mariah

I can usually scroll through my feed and find a little entertainment, but the well is a bit dry today. Maybe everyone is learning how tacky it is to air your dirty laundry on social media. God, I hope not. How else will I spend my time if I'm not reading their tales of woe?

I scroll a little further down and spot an ad for a photography course. My thumb stays a bit too long as I go to scroll again, and the screen takes me to their business page. Fuck. Now every ad I see for the next week will be about photography. I close the app.

It's nice to have a day off from work, but I don't have anything to do. My life has become the definition of boredom. I wake up, wander around my small house for a few hours, binge some television, then go to sleep.

Alone.

It's not that I haven't tried dating, but the men I meet are just so disgusting. It seems everywhere I turn I come face to face with a cheating piece of shit, as if I have a sign on my head that labels me as an eternal side piece. I want to be someone's main course, and that means waiting until the right man comes along.

And that's what I do. I wait. I've stopped putting myself out there because I'm tired. Dating in today's market will exhaust even the most enthused woman, and I'm far from enthused anymore. If life could just put Mr. Right into my path, that would be great.

I check through my texts and spot a few party invites from work acquaintances, though I'm not sure why they bother inviting me. My party shoes went into the trash a long time ago, right around the time I got a phone call from my most recent ex's wife.

A text comes through from a coworker asking if I can cover her shift tomorrow. With a sigh, I agree. What else did I have planned? A little extra money never hurt anything either.

A groan leaves me when I see which shift she needs covered. I hate mornings.

I grab a pint of ice cream from the freezer and go back to scrolling on my phone. Someone got engaged. Someone's baby did something normal that they thought was special. And oh, look, a photography ad.

I roll my eyes and keep going, but the next ad catches my eye.

A man and woman pose by a lake, and the love practically shines in their eyes. I click the ad, more interested in seeing pictures of the mystery couple than the text on the screen. I'm taken to a business page for a photographer running a special on something called a stranger session. I find it hard to believe that these people had never met before these pictures were taken. I've been on enough blind dates to know that this sort of chemistry doesn't just happen. Mostly it's a lot of looking at your phone and asking awkward questions.

The terms and conditions fill the screen when I click the post, pushing the pictures further down. It costs nothing to take part in a stranger session as long as both parties agree that the photographer can use the photos as promo material. My thumb hovers above another link. This one will take me to a sign-up sheet, where I'll enter my information for the photographer's consideration.

I'm a glutton for punishment, so I click again.

Five minutes pass, and I've uploaded a photo and signed my name on the dotted line. I'd be lying if I said I wasn't a little excited. This opportunity gives me a reason to dress up a bit and look pretty, and if the guy they choose for me has a good personality and a nice smile, all the better. I'm halfway through a daydream about our first year of dating when my phone pings with a notification, and a follow-up email dashes my visions of the perfect man.

The photographer will only choose one lucky man and woman for the stranger session, and the deadline to sign up is six p.m. Winners will be notified over the next twenty-four hours. This means I'll be up against all the other women who signed up for this opportunity, but how many bored single women could there be?

Probably a lot.

"Too good to be true," I mutter as I shove my phone into my pocket.

I grab the small watering can from beneath my sink and fill it to the brim. As I take a turn around my living room and water each of my plants, I'm reminded of just how boring I am. Instead of a dog or a cat or even a fish, I have fucking plants for pets. I vow to take the next exciting opportunity that comes my way, no matter how scary or strange it is. Whatever life throws at me, I'll open my arms and catch it because I refuse to stay inside this lackluster box. It's time to live.

Chapter Three

Del

The wheel on my mouse clicks as I scroll online. I sat in front of my computer as soon as I got back from my run, and I'm mentally preparing myself to look up the stranger session Taylor mentioned. It can't be worse than those blind-dating games on television where strangers sit across from each other and awkwardly chat while looking like they'd rather be anywhere else. Or the moment as neither person says something funny enough to deserve it, yet both people force weird, pained laughter. I die inside at the thought alone, to be honest.

I find the photographer on Facebook and click the post about the stranger session. Blind-date photo shoots look deranged, even if the pictured couple is kind of cute. Reading through the post, I learn how it works.

Two people are set up for a photo shoot. They're blind-folded until the moment they get a look at the person they've been paired with. They could be beautiful, homely, nice, mean. Who the fuck knows? But that's not the worst part. You're expected to take *intimate* photos with each other. Like, couples photos. Handholding, kissing, longing-looks photos. I can't picture doing any of this with someone I just met.

I scroll further. The strangers are kissing, and it looks so natural, despite such an unnatural set up. Happiness and attraction radiate from the participants' faces. Just thinking about it forces a cold sweat onto my brow.

My face isn't capable of making my expression look that happy or comfortable if I'm not feeling it. If I'm not attracted to my partner, the photographer will paste our mutual embarrassment for all of the internet to see.

I'm too inexperienced for this. I grew up with very religious parents, and I didn't go on my first date until I was eighteen. My virginity remained intact until I was nineteen, but I was still a heathen in my parents' eyes because I didn't wait until marriage. In my defense, if I had listened to them, I would have been a virgin until I died.

Either way, it wasn't a particularly happy childhood, and I never had an outlet for my repressed anger and feelings. I'm surprised I didn't become a psychopath from being forced to mask my emotions growing up.

Maybe it affected my ability to love, and maybe that's why I'm so against dating now. Maybe I gave it the good old college try with Lisa. Maybe I knew all along how it would end up because I could never give her what she wanted. What she needed. Maybe that pushed her beneath another man.

The thought of that day heats my skin and turns my insides into a pressure cooker, boiling my organs until they feel like they'll explode. I focus on the screen again, and a calm feeling washes over me. I click the link and begin plugging my information into the sign-up sheet. The best way to get over someone is to get under someone else, right? I add my picture and without thinking, I click submit. Panic sets in almost immediately.

What did I do?

I can just decline if they happen to message me back. The picture I included wasn't my best. They'll only choose one guy among god knows how many, so I'm probably worried about nothing.

Let it go, I tell myself. *They won't contact you, and if they do, just say you entered by mistake. Don't worry, they won't pick you.*

No fucking way. I stare at the unread email in my inbox, but I can't bring myself to click it. Maybe only a handful of people signed up for such a weird fucking thing, so of course I was picked.

I exit the app on my phone and pretend I never saw it. I try not to let my anxiety get to me, but it burns through the plastic as I stare down at my device.

Fuck me.

I open my phone again and bring up my email once more. It stares back at me with big, bold letters.

Vehement Photography.

Subject: Blind date shoot.

I click it with the hope of it saying, *sorry, we have chosen other applicants.* But it doesn't. It congratulates me on being chosen for the free shoot. Great.

Thank you for applying to get a free photo shoot. Our blind-date shoots are our most

popular giveaways. This is an experience
you won't soon forget! We are currently
selecting your partner and will be in touch
as soon as possible. If for any reason you
have decided against participating, please
respond to this email so we can give the
next person an opportunity.

Now is the time to tell them to give the opportunity
away to anyone besides me, but instead of clicking reply, my
thumb hesitates over the link to their most recent shoot. I
click it and their website fills my screen.

My eyes dance as I absorb the pictures. A girl sits on a
man's lap, leaning over him and kissing him. They look in
love. They look happy. And something inside me wants
that. The affection. The attention.

And the ability to walk away afterward like nothing
magical just fucking happened.

Spending a few hours pretending to be in love might be
worth the risk of an awkward moment or two, and there's *no*
risk of getting my heart broken once I leave.

When I go back to my email, I don't decline. As much
as I hate to admit it—and as much as I will never admit it to
Taylor—I'm warming up to the idea. I'm beginning to
want it.

I read the email again. They're searching for my match,
but how do they determine my match? Is it someone whose
looks complement mine? What a shallow way to have a
blind date, even if it's just for a photo shoot. What kind of
face complements mine, I wonder? Can attraction be
picked this way? On the shallowest level?

You two look like you'd make pretty babies, so I

matched you both to each other. Flawless methodology. Can't wait.

But now I have to play the waiting game. Once they've chosen my partner, we just have to wait for another email outlining the time and place for the shoot. And when I pull off my blindfold, I'm supposed to make out with a complete stranger as if I love them.

What could go wrong?

Chapter Four

Mariah

I cinch my apron around my waist, tie the strings into a neat bow, and get ready to work the counter. A line of customers winds through the small area between the counter and the front door. Whoever designed this place had little faith in our popularity. Unfortunately for us workers, we pay the price for their lack of foresight.

Agitated murmurs drift from the growing crowd. They're always *so* pleasant before they've had their morning caffeine boost, and waiting in this packed space only makes them kinder by the time they reach the counter.

"Medium black," a man shouts before I can even activate my register.

I can't tell him to hold on and wait a goddamn second, so I just smile at him and let my anxiety eat away at me until the register finally chooses to wake up. I punch in a medium black coffee.

"Anything else with that?" I ask, my plastic smile still on full display.

"No, just make it fast," he says without looking me in the eye.

My mother always said you catch more flies with honey, but this asshole is full of piss and vinegar. When a customer acts like an impatient toddler and demands expedient service, I guarantee the exact opposite.

I take his payment and get to work on his order. As I grasp the lid and place it over the cup, my hand slips and I spill hot coffee all over myself. The apron catches most of it, but the hot liquid scalds my arms. I bite my lip to keep from screaming out. The asshole will have to wait twice as long for his coffee, which is my only consolation prize for enduring these second-degree burns.

My phone chimes in my pocket, alerting me to a text message and inciting more angry groans from the crowd.

Relax, people, I won't fucking check it. I'll just make a new coffee while the old one's still burning me.

I put a little pep in my step for the second try, but the man is nearly irate by the time I slide his cup across the counter. He snatches it up and glares at me. "I don't know why I bother coming here. The service is terrible, and the coffee isn't even that good."

A rude reply hovers on my tongue, but I swallow it and smile. "I apologize, sir."

He huffs and sips his coffee as he walks away. I hope it roasts every taste bud from his tongue.

By the time the morning rush ends, my black hair falls from my ponytail, more coffee spills soak my clothes, and I only have the strength to lean against the counter and sigh.

"Hey," my manager says. "If you need a break, go ahead and take ten."

Thank fuck.

I rip off the apron and rush outside to my car. I'm

pretty sure I have an old shirt in there, and I'm more than ready to escape the aroma of old coffee. Rifling through the disaster that resides on the floorboard, I find a large t-shirt with a few paint stains on the front. The apron will cover those, and at least it's dry. I'll change once I go back inside.

My phone dings again, and I remember the missed message from earlier. I pull it from my pocket and stare down at the notification. It's an email from Vehement Photography, and the subject line makes my stomach tighten.

I've been chosen for a stranger session.

Sweat slicks my hands, and my stomach completes a barrel roll into my chest. This is so outside my comfort zone. I grew up in a time when stranger danger was all the rage on after-school specials. Now I've signed up to meet an unknown man and make out with him while someone takes pictures. For all I know, he could be a complete pervert, or even that asshole from this morning.

The options are endless. And terrifying.

I open the email and read through the text. They've already found my match, and the location and time of the photo shoot will be disclosed at a later date.

How nerve-wracking. Now I'm forced to stand on pins and needles while I wait for the next bit of information to trickle in. But even once I know where and when, I still won't know *who*.

Doubt begins to creep into my mind. What if my mystery man removes his blindfold and looks disappointed? What if *I'm* disappointed? How could I ever give the photographer the intimacy they hope for if we aren't attracted to each other?

I look down at my coffee-stained shirt and sigh. At this

moment, I don't feel very attractive, and I certainly don't feel like I deserve the coveted slot for this photo shoot.

I desperately want to feel something other than worthless. There has to be more for me than this. Some excitement and out-of-the-box experiences that can make me feel something more than numb.

Sliding my phone back into my pocket, I trudge into the coffee shop with my "clean" shirt in my hand. As I pass by nameless faces, I can't stop my brain from wondering if any of these men are *him*.

And they very well could be.

Against my will, my mind conjures up scenarios involving every strange man in the building. I imagine opening my eyes and seeing their faces for the first time, then being forced to kiss them. My stomach threatens to send up my breakfast each time. Maybe this wasn't such a good idea after all.

I head into the bathroom to change my shirt. Once I've situated my apron again, I pull out my phone and sit on the closed toilet seat. My fingers type out a quick reply to the email.

Sorry, I think I've changed my mind. You'll need to choose someone else. I appreciate the opportunity, and I apologize for any inconvenience.

My thumb hovers over the send button. But I can't do it.

I stand, shove my phone into my pocket, and return to the floor. My mother had another saying as well: Nothing ventured, nothing gained.

Chapter Five

Del

Gravel crunches beneath my tires as I drive down the longest, windiest road I've ever seen. It seems endless, but it's not. At the end waits a terrifying and hopefully exciting opportunity.

Shortly after I won the giveaway, I went through a period of self-loathing, insecurity, and overthinking. What if I'm not what my mystery girl is expecting? What if she can't hide the disgust on her face? Now I've landed on the final step: excitement.

My roommate would shit a brick if he knew the idea he came up with managed to somehow excite me. I still haven't told him. I can't let him think he had a good idea, can I?

The buildup to this moment hasn't been easy, though. The nervous energy of meeting a stranger had traveled straight to my fingertips, and I nearly had to restrain myself so I wouldn't hack into Vehement Photography's system and see my match ahead of time. But I didn't do it. I forced myself to put my tech knowledge aside and let the blind date remain . . . well, blind.

The trees begin to open up around the road, showing signs of habitation. My GPS signals that I'm here, and I pull into a driveway. Fall leaves cover the pavement in hues of reds and yellows. They crunch beneath my feet as I get out of my car.

The home is a gorgeous A-frame that looks like something out of a magazine. I suddenly feel insecure that I still live in a shitty two-bedroom apartment with a roommate. I take a step back toward my car, sabotaging myself before we even begin.

A melodic voice floats from the house and stops my backward progression. "Del Monroe?"

The woman waves at me from her wrap-around porch. A camera hangs around her neck, its gaping glass eye pointed at the ground. Soon she will aim it at me, and it will see everything.

Every facial movement.

Every unspoken word.

Every hidden emotion.

The camera doesn't lie, after all, and it's going to speak my truth loud and clear.

It's too late to run, so I walk toward her. She offers her hand, and I take it.

"Yes, I'm Del. You're Sarah, right?"

"I am! Nice to meet you. We're just waiting on your date, so come inside and settle your nerves."

I don't know if everyone arrives inherently nervous or if she sees the anxiety oozing from my widened eyes, but I hope it's the former. I'm not normally such a nervous man, but this situation is bringing it out of me.

I follow Sarah inside and realize how completely her work consumes her. Photographs spill over every surface. Antique cameras line the tops of the double bookcases in her living room, but the shelves hold no books. Instead, framed pictures fill each rectangular space. They mostly showcase nature shots, and they're very good.

As we enter the kitchen, I pick up a few of the pictures lying on the table. I sift through them, unable to tell if these are from other blind date photo shoots or if they show organic couples who've been dating for years. The connection is that believable.

I can't help but wonder if the couple creates this chemistry or if it's mostly due to the person operating the camera. Could she make two enemies look in love if captured in the right patch of sunlight?

It's possible.

Sarah slides a piece of paper across the worn oak surface and taps her finger above two lines near the bottom of the contract. "I just need your signature here and here. It's your standard photography release. In a nutshell, it basically says I can use your images for promotional material without compensating you, and you agree you won't contact the other participant once this is over. If you'd like to read through it, though, take your time."

This gives me a hint of relief. If things go poorly, I never have to worry about hearing from my blind date again. Some of the pressure has been taken off, so maybe I won't have a hard time pretending to like the woman if I really don't. It's not as if I'll have to endure another minute with her once the camera clicks for the final time.

I fill each blank with my information and pass it back to her without studying the fine print. If you've read one contract, you've read them all. She checks it over, tucks it into a leather laptop bag, and brings me into a smaller room.

A large window overlooks the backyard. Golden fields stretch into the distance, and a few trees dot the sprawling landscape. An old-fashioned swing hangs from one of the outstretched tree limbs. Two thick cords of rope lead down to the weathered board seat. Picturesque is an understatement.

Sarah follows my gaze to the backyard. "We usually set up at a local park for these shoots, but they were too crowded for what I wanted to do today. I figured you wouldn't mind having the shoot here. Thanks for being flexible."

"No problem."

She raises her camera to her eye, then fusses with a few of the buttons below the viewing screen. "Once Mariah gets here and signs her paperwork, you'll both be blindfolded and led outside. Then the fun can really begin." She offers me an excited smile.

Mariah. That's *her* name. And it's a pretty name, at that.

"You just have to stay in this room," she says. "If you come out of that door before we've put the blindfold over your eyes, the shoot is off. Your clothes are in the closet. We'll be in to go over last looks before we blindfold you."

I nod and she rushes out and leaves me with my thoughts. They grow more pessimistic the longer I wait. As each second stretches out as I dress, I struggle to keep my feet from turning toward the door and breaking into a run. Maybe I can sneak out before anyone else arrives.

But the thought of disappointing this girl I've never fucking met holds me in place. Yeah, I'd feel better, but at what cost to someone else? The poor girl would feel so awkward and unwanted if she arrived and found her partner had jumped ship. Then a thought strikes me as I look at my watch.

What if I'm the one who's been stood up?

Chapter Six

Mariah

I shift on my feet. Left, right, left, right. My toes curl in my shoes and a light sweat slicks my forehead. I can't see anything through the black blindfold wrapped around my head. Is it ruining my hair or smearing my makeup? I hope not. Sarah and her crew spent a lot of time styling and perfecting my look.

Ugh, the nausea is something else. My stomach twists into knots, looping and rolling until I feel sick. I almost didn't come, but the thought of what I could miss out on outweighed the fear of disappointment from either party.

A chill breeze brushes over my cheeks. Since I can't see anything, my ears work double time to provide sensory information. Leaves rustle somewhere nearby. Steps thud against the earth and grow silent. Fabric moves against skin in front of me, followed by more footsteps.

"We're almost ready, you two," Sarah says.

Every muscle in my body tenses. They may be almost ready, but I'm not. Now I want to rip off this blindfold and run for my car. I'd probably apologize on my way out for wasting everyone's time.

Someone breathes behind me. Each intake of air comes too fast, too ragged. It must be my match, because I'm breathing the same way.

"This is fucking terrifying," I whisper.

He chuckles. "It sure is."

Feet shuffle through the grass behind me, and then his back presses against mine. The warmth comforts me. Another breeze blows past us and carries his scent into my nose. Hints of cedar and bergamot make me dizzy, and I begin to think this might not be so bad after all. If I find him unattractive, I'll just close my eyes and focus on this scent.

"We're ready," Sarah says. "Turn to each other, but don't remove your blindfolds yet."

On wobbly legs, I turn around. The ground spins beneath me. I'm not sure if my nerves make it so hard to tell which way is up or if the blindfold has something to do with my sudden lack of balance, but I stumble forward.

Powerful arms catch me before I land in the dirt. Embarrassment tries to worm its way into the mix of emotions, but I'm too caught up in the feel of him to notice. My hands fill with his biceps. They flex against my palms, and I want to melt.

The camera shutter clicks several times in quick succession and draws me out of this blinding haze. I'd almost forgotten I'm standing in a spotlight, where every action and facial expression will be documented.

"Remove your blindfolds on three. One . . ."

I release his arms and reach behind my head.

"Two . . ."

I unfasten the tie and hold the loose ends between my shaking fingers.

"Three."

I pull the blindfold away.

A smile crosses my lips at the sight of him tugging the blindfold off his head in one motion. His dark blond hair sits in a mess on his head, and his piercing blue eyes nearly make my heart stop.

With a bite of his full lower lip, he eyes me, starting at my hair and moving down to my lips. Then his gaze roves lower. Straight to my cleavage. It's a typical guy move, but I can't deny that I like the way I feel beneath his scrutiny.

My nerves begin to recede. This date has nothing to do with my personality or likes and dislikes. The success of this moment is determined by how our bodies respond to each other.

My attention moves to the hard bulges that make up his muscular chest and the curves of his strong arms beneath his dark dress shirt. My gaze drops lower, to the outline of his cock through his slacks.

He's hard. For me. *Because* of me.

I'd say our bodies are responding pretty well, which makes me nervous all over again.

And excited.

Del

I've never seen such a beautiful creature. Wavy black hair frames her face and falls past her shoulders. Bright-blue eyes peer up at me. A bead of sweat gathers on the curve of her cleavage and drips between her full breasts. A purple dress clings to her in all the right places, and I can only imagine ripping it off with my teeth. The color matches the purple lines running through my dress shirt.

I'm so wrapped up in this vision of a woman that I hardly hear the click of the camera. If they hoped I'd look fucking in love with her, I'm sure they got their wish.

I adjust my stance when I see her eyes on my cock. Yes, I'm hard. Aching. Mind-bendingly starved to get my hands and my mouth on her. The only thing that would stop me would be if she uttered the safe word: autumn. The shoot ends immediately if either of us so much as whisper that word.

I hope she doesn't, because I sure as fuck will not.

"Hi," she says with a shy wave.

"Hi." I offer an equally awkward wave of my hand. This is painful, but not enough to make me say that word.

I tug at the long sleeves on my arms. They cover most of my tattoos, but the one on my neck creeps from the collar. Speaking of my collar, why does it feel so tight all of a sudden? I reach up and tug it away from my skin so I can get some air.

"Del, this is Mariah," Sarah says. "Mariah, this is Del."

Mariah chuckles. "Like the computer?"

"D-E-L." My cheeks heat.

Sarah lowers the camera and studies us. "Okay, Mariah, why don't you get a little closer? He doesn't bite."

Or do I? Because right now, I can think of a few places on her body I'd love to nip.

Mariah steps into me, and my heart rate quickens as her hands find mine. The warmth of her skin burns me, and I'm tempted to pull away from her touch, but the flirt in her eyes helps me tolerate the heat.

"Lean in nice and close, Mariah," Sarah says.

And she does. Her breath washes over me as her mouth draws closer to mine. She smells like citrus and strawberries.

Without waiting for the next prompt, I lean in the rest of the way and take her mouth. My lips spread on hers. She accepts my tongue, and the camera shutter clicks away like a thousand microscopic firecrackers.

Mariah whimpers as my hands rise up her sides and land on her neck. My fingertips graze her hairline, and I'm tempted to get all up in there and give her something to really whimper over. But I keep my cool.

"What do you like?" I whisper against her lips.

"I like having my earlobes touched."

That's a new one for me, but I go for it. My fingers leave her hairline and land on the lobes of her ears. As I caress the soft skin, her perfect lips part to release a low moan. I sure hope they caught *that* on camera.

"And what do you like?" she whispers.

"I like my hair pulled."

Her hand goes right for my hair, and an absolutely feral groan leaves my lips as she grips the strands and pulls.

Click, click, click, click.

When I open my eyes, a beaming smile lights her face. This playful look draws something playful out of me as well. But something malevolent too. A part of me I've never confronted.

I'm clinically obsessed with thoughts beyond this moment. Thoughts of her beneath me as I make sure she knows she's mine. Absolutely no one else's.

Mine.

And the camera flashes again.

Chapter Seven

Mariah

It's cool outside, but the heat rushing from his fingertips burns me. They light me on fire wherever they land on my body. He sits on a bench and pulls me onto his lap, so I straddle him beneath the colorful fall foliage. My mouth hovers over his as the camera clicks to the rapid tempo of my heartbeat.

His fingers wind through my hair as he looks up at me with more need than I've ever seen in a man's eyes. It's as if he believes my lips can provide his next breath. He adjusts beneath me, and his erection presses against me. My cheeks flush with heat.

"I'm sorry," he whispers.

"Don't apologize. I'm grinding on your lap," I say with a nervous laugh.

I understand why he's turned on. I am too. The wetness between my legs can't be controlled when his hands move over my body or his mouth lands on mine. Add that to this extremely intimate position and his rock-hard cock beneath me. The lust is only intensified by the fact that I can't sleep with him. We signed a contract stating we'd part ways after this and retain our anonymity.

I thought that was a good idea at the time. It makes it easier to act like I like someone if I know I'll never have to see them again. But this isn't an act.

"Do you like to be on top or bottom?" he asks, and those words cause a confused hurricane of feelings inside me. Between my legs.

"Bottom."

He lifts me, camera flashing to the left of us, and lays me down in the cold grass. He places his hips between my legs and leans over me. My chest rises and meets his. The cool fall air assaults my lungs, but then he kisses me, those full lips capturing mine. The camera's furious clicks fade away, and it's just us.

His hips push against me, and his hard length strains against his pants. I long to shed our clothes and give this photographer and her assistant more than they bargained for. Which is very unlike me. I usually don't even kiss on the first date.

What is this man doing to me?

His mouth moves to my ear, and he captures the delicate skin between his teeth. Applying just the right amount of pressure, he teases me until I'm pliable putty in his hands. I've genuinely forgotten about the two onlookers when I hear the snap of the photographer's fingers beside my head.

"Hey, you two! I'm glad you're both caught up in the spirit of things, but this isn't the best angle for the shots I want. Let's try something else."

I don't want to try something else. I want to keep doing exactly what we're doing. Unless the something else involves moving to a bedroom and ripping our clothes off, I'd rather stay right where I am.

But Del climbs off me and stands up, and I can't remember the last time I felt so unattached from something. For a moment, we were connected by some invisible thread woven between us. Now Sarah has snipped it apart, and I'm slightly annoyed. I get to my feet anyway, curious to see what she has planned for us next.

Del

Sarah turns to her assistant. "Sam, remember that pose we did with the last couple?"

He pulls a bottle of eye drops from his pocket and drips the liquid into his eyes, then nods.

"It didn't quite work for them because they lacked the right look, but I think it's perfect for these two." She turns to us. "Sam will show you how you'll pose, Del. Mariah, you just go with the flow, okay?"

We nod, but I don't like this. The assistant is a rugged fuck boy who gives me a run for my money in looks. He also reminds me of the guy I caught beneath my ex. My jaw clenches as Mariah moves toward him.

Sam wraps her hair around his hand, sits on the bench, and pulls her onto his lap with such fucking finesse. I want to abandon all composure and bludgeon him with Sarah's camera, but I take a deep breath, calm myself the fuck down, and watch.

I don't like the way his hands move on her body. He

looks at her like he's ready to devour her. I mean, I get it. She's fucking beautiful, and she's a natural for photos.

But for the duration of this photo shoot, she's mine.

"Okay, I got it," I say as I step toward them. I wrap my hand around Mariah's arm to help her to her feet and put some space between them.

"Get your hand off her." Sam gets to his feet, nearly sending Mariah to the ground.

I release her once I'm sure she's steady, and then I step into Sam. He might be a match in looks, but I could beat his ass with one arm tied behind my back. "I think you've forgotten your place, Mr. Assistant."

"Del! Sam! Both of you need to relax!" Sarah yells as she gets between us. "Everyone take five!"

I brush a hand through my hair and step away from the fuck boy. "I'm going to have a smoke."

He scoffs and pulls the eye drops from his pocket again. *Your eyes are moist enough,* I think, but I keep the snarky comment to myself and head to my car. I grab a cigarette and lighter from the center console. The nicotine should take the edge off. I fucking hope.

I may have overreacted a bit, but I couldn't let him continue to touch her like that. Maybe I was only imagining it, but she didn't seem as comfortable as she did with me. Instead of leaning into him, she'd leaned away. That had driven my need to get her away from the handsy assistant, though a bit of jealousy may have played a part.

I light the cigarette and lean back against my car. I never expected to feel like this when I signed up for the photo shoot. The feelings weren't supposed to be so real, especially not this quickly.

Gravel crunches near my car, and I turn toward the sound. Mariah walks toward me and holds out her hand, wiggling her fingers and signaling for me to give her a cigarette. I hand one to her and light it for her.

"Sorry for grabbing you," I say.

She shrugs and takes a drag. "I'm glad you stepped in. That guy was making me pretty uncomfortable. You got a little jealous, though, huh?" A smirk tips the corner of her mouth upward.

I scoff. "No," I say, but it's a lie. I sure as fuck did get jealous. Very jealous.

"I think you did."

I turn and step into her until her back presses against the car. "Maybe I did. So what? Your body belongs to *me* for the duration of this photo shoot, doesn't it?" My hand drops to her hip and squeezes.

She exhales a breath filled with smoke, and the smile on her face makes me rock-hard again. "I didn't think I'd like control like that, but here we are."

My hand winds through her hair, and I tighten my hold near her scalp. I crane her neck and press my mouth against her throat, where I bite and suck until I leave a mark on her. "Now that fuck will know who you belong to," I whisper against her skin.

Where is this coming from? What about this girl is bringing this out of me?

And how will I say goodbye when the shoot is over?

Chapter Eight

Mariah

My cheeks flush when I glance over at Sarah's assistant, and I swear his bloodshot eyes have glued themselves to the hickey on my neck. I'm not embarrassed, though. Just incredibly turned on. I never thought I would like feeling owned or marked like I'm a piece of meat instead of a human. But here I am, soaked from it.

"Everyone good?" Sarah asks as she raises her camera and starts mashing buttons. She doesn't look at us as she speaks.

Del and I nod.

He hasn't looked at the assistant since we all gathered in the backyard again. If you had asked me before this moment if I'd like someone who became possessive of me, I'd tell you no thanks. But for some strange reason, I *really* like it today. I love occupying the part of this man's mind that makes him feral over me.

I know it's not healthy. He's essentially waving a giant

red flag toward me. But after this shoot, I'll never see him again, so I'll let that fucking flag wave in my face.

Del sits on the bench, just like Sarah's assistant had. He pulls me onto his lap like Sam did, but he takes it a step further and lifts my thigh so that my back curves. Then his hand winds through my hair, and he pulls me to his mouth.

"Mine," he whispers against my lips.

My hips scoop forward, dragging my warmth over his erection, and he growls before pulling away. The camera springs to life as Del's lips find mine again. Each rapid click of the shutter matches my heartbeat, and I wonder if the camera will capture this intangible passion between us. The warmth traveling from his lap and gliding through my body. The need and hunger racing through our veins. I've never wanted anyone so badly as I want this man at this moment.

But we can't.

And that only makes me want him more.

"I think we've covered the steamy portion of the session. Let's take some final sweet shots." Sarah motions toward the woods. "Walk toward the tree line holding hands."

We get up, interlace our fingers, and head toward the trees. He grips my hand harder, a smirk tugging at his lips.

"Okay, stop and give me something romantic," Sarah calls behind us.

We turn to each other beneath a splash of fall color offered by the tree canopy. It's really fucking romantic. His hand rises to my cheek and loops behind my ear. He rubs the tender lobe between his thumb and pointer finger. I whimper. It's like my earlobe goes right to my vagina. Not even rubbing my nipples turns me on this much.

And he remembered what that touch would do to me. Not many men take the information women give them and actually use it, but he's making use of it now.

He leans in and puts his forehead to mine.

Sarah squeals with excitement behind her camera. "That's it, guys! This is great!"

A grumble comes from her assistant, but he can't break this spell we're under. Something incredible passes between Del and me. A spark. A longing for more. That's why what Sarah says next drives an invisible fist into my stomach.

"Okay, I think we have enough shots to go through. You guys are done!"

There's an instant emptiness when he pulls away. My hands long to pull him against me again, to feel his breath on my skin once more, but I stay still and offer a weak smile.

"Have a good day, Mariah," Del says.

My heart breaks as he hurries away, leaving me feeling completely abandoned. I didn't expect him to stick around, but my stomach sinks at the speed with which he rushes toward his car. Maybe I didn't affect him as strongly as he affected me—though his raging erection says otherwise.

"Bye, I guess," I whisper, too low for anyone else to hear.

Del

I pull onto the main road as a hurricane of thoughts whips through my mind. Mariah had looked so lost as I pulled away from her, but I had to leave as quickly as I could after Sarah said we were done. I wouldn't have stuck to the contract if I'd stayed around a moment longer.

I wanted her. I *still* want her. Even as my car reaches

town, I can't stop thinking about her or the smell of her skin. A sweet, fruity scent that lingers inside me. She infiltrates my body and takes over my mind.

And she can't. She absolutely fucking can't.

I light a cigarette to drown out her scent, but not before pulling my shirt to my nose and getting one more hit of her. I'm hoping the heat of possession cools by the time I get to my house. This just isn't normal. No one should feel this way toward another person after meeting them once. But most people don't meet a person for the first time and get to have their hands and mouth all over them.

This situation is unique. But equally shitty.

I pull into my driveway and hope Taylor isn't home. I really don't want him to ask any questions. Despite my hope, I nearly collide with him when I head into the house.

"How was it?" he asks.

I throw him a death glare.

He puts his hands out to shield himself from my silent wrath. "That bad?"

He doesn't know I went to the photo shoot. He thinks he annoyed me enough that I went on a regular date.

"No, it was too good."

His head cocks. "I'm not following. If it went well, why do you look so damn angry?"

"Because I went and did one of those asinine blind date photo shoots. The stranger session."

A shit-eating grin walks across his face, just like I expected.

"And it went great."

"So what the hell is the problem, dude?"

"I signed a contract that said I wouldn't see her again."

Taylor laughs, and it makes me want to punch him in the throat. "That has almost no legal standing, Del. How did you not know that? They can't keep you from seeing someone once you leave their property."

I pinch the bridge of my nose. I wish I'd thought about that before I cold-shouldered the fuck out of her. I wouldn't want to see me if I were her.

And how will I find her now? Aside from her first name and her earlobe kink, I know nothing about her. There wasn't much time for small talk. They kept the shoot so impersonal yet somehow super personal at the same time.

Frustration simmers in my gut, ready to boil over. The obsessive tug munches away at my insides. Despite the contract, despite knowing that it's a terrible idea, I know what I have to do to make this insatiable ache go away.

I have to find her.

Chapter Nine

Del

I drive on familiar roads with familiar landmarks. Similar trees welcome me as I travel toward the house in the woods. The normal part of my brain keeps waving a red flag, telling me to stop what I'm doing. The irrational part keeps lighting that fucking flag on fire. Regardless of which side is winning, the rational question remains.

What if she didn't use her real name?

I didn't find anyone named Mariah in our area. If she didn't lie on her paperwork, she either keeps a very private profile or she doesn't have social media. Who doesn't have social media these days? It's like she's a ghost.

If she's a ghost, then I'm being haunted by the taste of her. By the sound of her whimpers and moans. By the fruity scent that is so uniquely hers. I've become obsessed with that smell. My brain fabricates it in realistic clarity, and I chase it into a dead end every time.

I pull into the driveway and look around. The lights are

off, and no cars wait in the driveway. I couldn't have planned this more perfectly if I'd tried.

When I was here for the photo shoot, I didn't notice any cameras, so I push my hands into some gloves and head for the front door first. The doorknob doesn't twist, so I try the back door next. Still no luck, but the window beside the back door is open just a crack. I slide it along its track, grip the sill, and enter the house.

I pace through the shadows and try to remember where Sarah placed the contracts. I remember signing it, but not what she did with it afterward. Each doorknob twists beneath my gloved grasp, but I find no new leads. An empty bedroom. A walk-in pantry. The bathroom. The last room I try is her office.

Several kitted-out cameras sit on the desk. Pictures adorn a clothesline that drapes between the walls. My eyes catch on one of the photos beside me.

It's us.

My hand is buried in her hair, and the smile on my face makes me unrecognizable to myself. I don't think I've ever smiled like that before. And Mariah? Her dimples punctuate each cheek on either side of her giant smile. My eyes rove down the beautiful curve of her back on my lap. Fuck, it's beautiful.

She's beautiful.

And I like how I look beneath her.

I snatch down the picture and replace it with one of the loose photographs scattered on the desk before turning my attention to the filing cabinet beside it. I open a drawer and thumb through the papers inside until I land on pay dirt.

The contracts.

I go through each paper until I find ours, and then I write down her info on a notepad and pocket it. On my way out, I notice an eye drop bottle on the kitchen counter and remember Sarah's little *ass*-istant using it to wash the marijuana from his glassy eyes. Just the thought of that guy makes my blood boil again. I'm going to explode.

I need to leave before I do something I'll regret. All for Mariah. The woman who probably has no interest in seeing me ever again.

Mariah

I doodle on a napkin during the brief lull at work as my thoughts return to the photo shoot. It's rekindled a bit of my drive to draw again. I used to draw all the time, but then life at a mundane job got the best of me. I haven't picked up a pen to put it on paper to draw in at least a year. A coffee stain grows in the top right corner of my picture from a spill I didn't realize was there.

Fuck it. It adds to the picture.

The service bell rings, and I fold up the drawing and shove it into my pocket before returning to the counter to take orders. Once I've handed over the two black coffees, I recede into my mind again. But the creative fountain has ceased to flow.

Did I mention I hate this job? I don't even drink fucking coffee.

The bell dings again, and I hurry to fill yet another order. I don't even bother to look at the man's face. After so long, they all seem to blur together anyway.

"Thanks," the man says as I slide his drink across the counter.

The voice stops me from moving away. I look up and see a face that matches the familiarity of the voice. His dark eyes rove down my stained apron.

"Y-you're welcome," I say, like an idiot.

"Do you remember me?"

My cheeks flush. "Yes, from the photo shoot."

"Sam," he says as he pulls a bottle of eye drops from his pocket and proceeds to use them in a fucking coffee shop.

It's that creepy assistant from the photo shoot. I lick my lips, tuck a strand of hair behind my ear, and force a smile onto my face. "It was nice to see you again, Sam, but I gotta get back to work. Sorry!"

I rush away before he can say anything else.

He's not unattractive, but I'm not interested. Even if he didn't creep me out, I don't have time to be interested. Besides, the whole interaction between Del and him made me uncomfortable. Well, uncomfortable because it made me want Del more. Until he pulled a one-eighty on me and became an asshole who could hardly say goodbye before he left. I'm not sure what I did to anger him, and I never intend to find out.

When I turn around, Sam is gone. Thank God.

"That guy left this for you," my coworker says, handing me a picture. It's the image of me on his lap, and on the back is his phone number. I can't dodge the weird glance from my colleague.

I slip the picture into my pocket and rush into the back to avoid her gaze and let the uncomfortable interaction wash away from me so I can finish up the rest of this shitty shift and go home. I can wallow better there.

Chapter Ten

Del

With her full name and address, I figured out she works at a bougie coffee shop downtown. I'm watching the place from my parking spot on the road when I see that skeezy assistant walking out of there. My fingers tighten around my steering wheel when I see the smarmy smile on his weasel face.

Why is he here? Is she seeing him? She never signed a contract agreeing she wouldn't socialize with his stupid ass, so it's possible.

I smack the wheel. *Fuck.*

He passes the car without seeing me, and I breathe a sigh of relief. I don't want Mariah to know I'm watching her. That would be fun to explain.

I hate the feelings she's stirred up inside me. This is something I didn't even feel with my ex. I just want to be around her. Breathe the same air as her. Exist in the same place as her. This woman has consumed me.

I pull onto the street and drive home. Maybe once I get

back to the house, I can find something to occupy my mind long enough to give me a break from this torment.

But nothing seems to work. I try to binge something on Netflix, but I spend more time flipping through the selections than actually watching anything. A new game came out on PC, and I've been dying to play, but it doesn't hold my attention. It feels as if everything I do is just to pass the time until I can see her again, but that will never happen. Well . . . unless I make it happen.

An idea forms in my mind, and I grab my keys and set off again. The clock ticks toward midnight. I should be in bed, but there's no way I can sleep until I do this. My skin feels too tight, and my mind races with images of her face. It's as if each click of the camera shutter has deposited the photos of that day directly into my brain.

I grip the wheel, turn onto her street, and watch the windows of each house I pass. I search for any sign that someone might be awake—the flicker of a television, an office light left on as someone burns the midnight oil—but the entire neighborhood seems to be sleeping.

Which is good. I wouldn't want anyone to report what I'm about to do.

After I cut my headlights, I pull against the curb near her house. I can only hope she doesn't have a camera aimed at this side of the street. Most people use those doorbell cameras these days, and I should be out of the way if she has one.

Pulling gloves onto my hands, I exit the car and walk along the side of the house. Not even the crickets are out tonight. My feet slide through the dewy grass, and I'm grateful she keeps a clean yard so I don't have to worry about crunching through dead leaves. I find her back door unlocked, so I let myself in.

The lights are off. I feel along the wall, trying to find her bedroom. I'm drawn to one specific door, like her life force is calling mine. I stop and touch the knob with a gloved hand, and my heart thumps against my chest as it turns in my grasp.

A night light casts a purple glow beside the bed. It's the only illumination in the room. She faces away from me, and her long, dark hair drapes over the pillow beneath her head. On silent feet, I creep to the side of the bed and remove my glove so I can run my bare fingertips through those strands. She can't feel it, but I can.

The sheet hugs her body, and my eyes snag on every delicious curve. My cock strains against the zipper holding it back. As if they have been taken over by some unseen entity, my hands move toward the sheet. I long to pull it back and see what's hidden beneath it, but panic strangles me. I stop. If she woke up and saw me, everything would be over before it's had a chance to begin. Any hope of getting closer to her would be ripped away.

As I return my hands to my sides, my gaze jumps to her en suite bathroom. Another small night light brightens the space above the sink. Is my little venti girl afraid of the dark?

I sneak into the bathroom and look around the room. I *need* to come, and I don't want to come on her. Not yet.

My eyes lock on the tube of moisturizer sitting on the sink by the soap dispenser. When I untwist the cap, my cock throbs at the thought of what I could do. I want to come in her lotion so she has to put me on her skin.

Wear me.

I free my cock and begin to stroke myself. My mind wanders to dirty thoughts of her as I lean back against the counter and stare at the pure perfection lying on the bed. I imagine what it would be like to spread her legs and bury my face in her warmth. I want to coat my tongue and chin in her arousal.

I wonder what her pussy looks like as I stroke faster. How does she feel? Tight, I bet. Warm and fucking wet. Just the thought of her tightens my balls. I hold the moisturizer's opening against the head of my cock, ensuring the hole is positioned so that I don't waste a single drop. With clenched teeth, I stifle a groan as I fill the bottle with my come.

Once I've screwed the cap onto the tube again, I shake it up and mix everything together. When she next flips open the cap, she won't be any wiser. I hope she likes wearing me. My scent mixes well with hers.

On my way out of her room, I spot a notebook and her laptop on the desk. I look back at the bed and make sure she's still asleep before opening her computer. It hums to life without a password, which isn't very smart. Everyone should lock their computers with a password. But I should be grateful, because it makes what I do next that much easier.

I plug in the flash drive that's been burning a hole in my pocket. This is the whole reason I came here. Coming in her lotion was just a side road I couldn't help but take. I attach the flash drive to the adapter and plug it into her phone next. I'll be able to track everything now. And be able to see if she's talking to that fucking assistant—or anyone else.

I'm about to leave, but curiosity gets the better of me and I open the notebook. Plain white pages stare back at me as I flip through from back to front, but then I land on something she's drawn. This is a sketchbook.

Using the light from the computer screen, I study the picture with a smile on my face. She's drawn a maple tree with a bench beneath it, and on that bench sits a camera.

She's not only beautiful. She's talented, too. And she's been thinking of that day as often as I have, apparently.

I pull out my phone and snap a picture of the drawing. I have plans for this.

My mission complete, I head for the door, but not before turning to catch a final glimpse of her shape beneath the sheet. "Goodnight, venti."

Chapter Eleven

Mariah

The shower is my favorite part of my mornings. It's a chance to refresh and energize my body and mind. The detachable shower head with the pulse setting isn't so bad either. For my tired muscles, of course.

I get out and wrap a towel around me. Once I dry myself off, I pick up my moisturizer, flip open the cap, and squirt it into my hands. The creamy white substance wafts its usual fruity scent up to my nose, but there's a hint of something else. The mildest smell I can't place. I don't mind it though, and I continue to rub it into my skin.

My phone buzzes, and I walk over to grab it off the nightstand. An unknown number stares up at me.

Hey.

Who is this?

My mind flashes to the picture with Sam's number on the back. I didn't put it into my phone because I'm not interested. I grab my discarded pants and pull the folded picture from the pocket. I verify the matching numbers with a sigh.

Now I'm just annoyed. I don't want anything to do with him. I don't want anything to do with anyone who was at that fucking photo shoot.

I send the message and toss my phone onto the bed. I wish I'd never signed up for that stupid stranger session.

It's bad enough that I'm still thinking about Del, even after he was such an asshole toward me, but now I've collected a creepy stalker. What sort of energy do I give off that would attract the worst kinds of men?

My brain superimposes Del into the stalker position, and I can't deny the way that combination makes me feel. Why couldn't it have been this way? If Del had been the stalker and Sam had been the asshole, life would be so much simpler. We'd all get what we want.

I close my eyes and imagine what it would be like to be hunted by Del. And what it would be like once he caught me. We could play out my secret fantasy I've never shared with anyone. Well, anyone aside from the randos on a fetish site I sometimes frequent. But they don't know my identity, and that stuff never goes further than a little roleplay and rubbing one out on my own.

But what if it could be different?

Maybe I need to pay the site a visit. If nothing else, at least it will get my mind off of my current situation. I open my laptop and navigate to the site.

Del

The fucking assistant texted her. She clearly wasn't interested, which is good, but I have to look into this guy. I search his name and come up empty, but then I search his number and find out everything I need to know.

It's linked to a different name, but when I look up that name, the age matches. It also comes up with a nice rap sheet and a mugshot. Roger Mathy. Thirty. Convicted sexual predator for sexual assault perpetrated on a female victim younger than fourteen.

What an absolute piece of shit.

Does his boss know about his disgusting past? Would she let him pull girls onto his lap if she did?

Fuck that guy. Maybe I should let Sarah know who she hired.

A notification pops up on my laptop. Mariah has signed onto a fetish site, it seems. I mirror her screen and see her typing in a chat. What is my little venti girl doing here?

Whorista: 25/f/ny

I split my screen and search for the website, then create an account. With a few more keystrokes, I'm in the chat with Mariah. Replies fly on the screen, pushing her message further up the board, and I can only hope I catch her eye.

ItsVenti: 27/m/ny

Not my best username, but it's all I could think of. Lately the name venti is always on my mind, just behind hers. It's that silly little coffee shop she works at. Every time I go there to learn her schedule, that word stares at me.

A private message pops up. It's Mariah.

Whorista: Where in NY?
ItsVenti: Upstate, you?
Whorista: Same.
ItsVenti: What are you looking for on here?

Little bubbles appear on the screen, bouncing up and down as she types a reply for far too long. She's probably typing, deleting, and typing again. Anticipation slicks my palms with sweat. What will she say?

Whorista: I think I have a stalker...

Yeah she does. It's me. But I don't think she means me. I left no sign of my presence in her house . . . unless she discovered my gift in her moisturizer. That's highly unlikely. I mixed it well.

Could one girl be unlucky enough to have two stalkers at once?

I type a reply.

ItsVenti: You think you have a stalker, so you go on a kink chatroom?

Whorista: I like how the fear is making me feel. I think he was watching me at my job this evening. I don't know why, but it made me ache.

My excitement dissipates. She's talking about the child predator, not me. She has no idea that I've been watching her too. The rational side of me wants to tell her to call the police. Tell them. But then they might find me too.

Whorista: I don't like the guy that's stalking me, though. I keep picturing someone else instead, and that's getting me too worked up.

A warm wave of relief washes over me.

ItsVenti: You want to be scared?

Whorista: I think I do.

ItsVenti: How scared? Like, chased through the woods kind of scared?

The lack of response on her end worries me. I go back to the mirrored screen and hack into her webcam. When she pops onto my screen, I find out why she's not responding.

A crumpled towel wraps around her midsection, leaving her beautiful breasts exposed. Her hair is still damp from a shower. With her left hand, she twists her nipple between her fingertips, but her right hand rests in her lap beneath the towel. I don't need her to respond to know she wants me to keep going.

ItsVenti: And what happens when I catch you?

Mariah's mouth drops open, and she leans back a little further. Her legs spread and the towel falls away, giving me a clear view of her hand between her thick thighs.

ItsVenti: Would you struggle against me, or would you want it?

She's rubbing herself, but she uses her free hand to peck out a reply. The notification pops up on the screen.

Whorista: I would struggle. I would fight you with every-thing I have. But I would want it.

When I was younger, I watched a lot of CNC porn—a disgusting amount—so it's no surprise that my cock is rock hard at the thought of acting out my fantasy with her. It doesn't help that I can see those fine movements of Mariah's body as she rocks her hips to my words and chases an orgasm when she doesn't know I'm watching.

ItsVenti: You're into CNC?
Whorista: What's that?
ItsVenti: Consensual non-consent. You give all the consent to me beforehand, and I do whatever I want to your body. Up to your hard limits, of course. If I catch you, I fuck you until you can't stand, even if you beg me to stop.

She throws her head back and releases a feral moan as she rubs her clit. I had no clue the sweet girl on my lap for photos would be in a chatroom like this. That she'd be into something like this. I mean, she was into my dominance and jealous possession of her body. It's not that far of a leap to assume she might want to be fucked like she was a "thing" to use.

Whorista: I want that. So fucking bad.

I pull out my cock and stroke the heat of my length. I ache for her. I've never wanted anything more in my life.

ItsVenti: Praise or degradation?
Whorista: I don't know.
ItsVenti: Do you like being a good girl? Or a whore?
Her lips tighten at the question, and the movement between her legs stops. Have I pushed her too far?
Whorista: Can't I be both?
ItsVenti: You can be anything you want with me.
Whorista: When and where?

We come nearly in unison. Her trembling wanes just as mine begins. I stroke harder and faster. Come spills down my hand as she pulls her come-soaked fingers from between her legs. It could be my hand.
It *will* be mine.
And so will she.

Chapter Twelve

Mariah

Crickets chirp around me, though it's not even nighttime yet. They're pre-gaming, I think. The sun eases below the horizon, but there's still a little daylight left. Fall air nips at my skin, and I clutch my jacket closer to my body. The further I walk into the woods, the more I wonder if I'm doing the right thing.

I literally seduced a random stranger on the internet and told him I wanted to be hunted through the woods like an animal. What the fuck am I doing?

At least we have a safe word—pumpkin—if anything becomes too much for me. But do I even know what is too much for me? I feel like I won't know until the line is crossed, but I guess that's what a safe word is for.

I look around. The trees grow in thick clumps in this part of the woods, and I worry he won't be able to find me. We didn't exactly exchange contact information. Hell, we didn't even share our names. He wants me to call him "nightmare," and he'll be wearing a mask. He could be anyone beneath that mask. And by doing this, I'm willing to let *anyone* inside me.

What the fuck am I doing? I get a little bit of a stalker and suddenly I want to give myself away to the first person I meet on the internet? All because I kind of like how being stalked makes me feel between my legs?

The fear morphs into some strange arousal that I can't control. When Del got all possessive of me, it went right to my pussy, and I haven't been able to stop thinking about it. I'll just imagine this masked man is him. I might not feel as nuts if it's someone I know. But I might not enjoy it as much if it is.

I can't help but wonder what he's been up to since the photo shoot. Does he ever think of me, or, like the photos, was our meeting just a forgotten snapshot in time?

Wind kicks up, whipping my hair around and lifting my skirt. I hold the fabric against my legs. My thighs are cold, but my boots keep me warm. I worry I'll get lost if I venture too much further into the woods, so I stop by a large pine tree and wait.

An ominous whistle comes from somewhere behind me, and it's not the wind. "Run, little whore!" a deep, menacing voice shouts. "Run! Because when I catch you, I'm going to fuck you!"

The words rush to my ears and travel toward my lower belly, where they slowly meld with the growing warmth between my legs. I kick off the soft ground and start running. How did he find me so fast?

I pick up my pace through the woods, squeezing through trees along a path of my own making. Heavy foot-falls follow my every move, granting me the fear I've been chasing. Even though I set this up, even though I consented to all of it, my body doesn't seem to understand the lack of risk. My brain knows we're okay, but my body reacts in a panic.

Run, escape, and avoid getting fucked, no matter how much you want to be fucked. That's what my body screams to my brain.

My heartbeat races against my chest. It feels like it's trying to come out of my mouth but is stuck in my throat. I gasp past it and keep going until my legs begin to shake. I fall against a tree. I can't hear his footsteps anymore, and I hope I can take a moment to catch my breath.

"There you are," says a voice behind me.

I turn with a gasp, and my gaze lands on the glint of a knife. I didn't agree to weapons.

"Why do you have a knife?" I yell.

"To make you do what I want."

He doesn't need a weapon to do that. I agreed to do what he wants.

"Raise that skirt and rub your pretty little cunt for me," he says behind the mask. "I want to see you squirm against that tree."

Okay. Maybe this isn't what I fantasized about after all. This feels wrong. But I comply and lift my skirt because this is what I asked for. Essentially.

My eyes lock on the skull mask, then drop to the knife hanging at his side. My hand rides up my thighs before dipping into my panties and rubbing between my legs. Cold air tantalizes and teases me with each pass of my warm fingers.

"That's good. Come for me," he groans as he rubs against the bulge in his black pants.

I lean against the tree, my thighs trembling as I rub harder and faster. Quick, circular motions bring me closer to climax, and I close my eyes with every shudder of my body. As the wave finally crashes between my legs, my lids clench shut. When I open them again, the man is gone, as if he was never there to begin with. If it weren't for the imprints of his shoes where he stood, I'd think I imagined the whole thing.

Another whistle punctuates the stale fall air. It sounds so far away, but it's a sound that makes my blood heat and my heart race.

Run.

Del

I find the blinking dot on my phone and follow it. The whistles are a mind game to let her know I'm here and that I'm searching for her.

Hunting her.

The pinging dot grows and grows as I near her. Eventually I'm close enough that I don't need my phone any longer. I can feel her.

Breathe her in.

Sense her.

"Run, run, my little whore!" I shout. I want her to feel my words in her bones. I want my voice to echo in her ears long after I speak.

Her footsteps sound from my right, and I take off after her. I can't wait to catch her and put her beneath me. I long to feel what I've *dreamed* of and obsessed over since the moment I felt her on my lap.

Her dark hair blows backward as she runs, whipping in

the wind. She looks feral. Like a wild animal attempting to escape a larger, wilder animal. How fitting.

"Are you scared yet? Afraid of what I'll do to your pussy once I catch you?" I yell.

She answers with a breathless whimper.

"I'm going to rip you limb from limb with my cock. Tear your legs apart and take you!"

She's getting tired. Her feet hit the earth harder with every step. The gap between us is closing, which means less and less space between my mouth and hers.

Then I remember this fucking ghost mask. I can't kiss her because I can't let her see my face. She agreed to let the unknown nightmare chase her, not me.

Not Del.

She's so close now. I'm near enough to hear each strained intake of breath, and then I round a tree and spot her. I leap forward and wrap my hand around her arm, halting her forward momentum.

A blood-curdling scream tears from her throat and almost makes me release her, but I remind myself that this is what she wants. I push her to the ground and climb on top of her. Even as she flails and struggles beneath my weight, this is exactly what she asked for.

"Stop!" she screams. "Please."

I pin her arms above her head and grip her wrists. She strains and bucks beneath me, and I smell the scent of her genuine fear. This isn't the way I wanted to experience her for the first time, but it's this or nothing. I'll take whatever she'll give me.

"Shh. Let your nightmare fuck you," I growl against her cheek.

"No! Don't!" she screams as I force her legs apart.

But she didn't say the safe word, so I keep going.

I rip the panties from her body. Nothing will keep me from her, and I want her to remember what I've done as she drives home with her bare ass against the seat of her car.

I pull down the front of my black sweatpants. My cock aches for the sweet, perfect pussy squirming in front of me. She writhes and strains as my cock presses against her slit. She's already creamy wet. As if she's already come.

"You're so wet," I growl as I fist my cock.

Her eyes widen at the sight of my piercing. I probably should have told her about the two black barbells on the underside of my cock, but I didn't think about it. It'll feel good inside her, though.

I draw back my hips and line myself up with her entrance. The moment I sink inside her, a strangled scream comes from her throat. Despite her pleas and begging, I push inside her because she never once says the word that can end this.

Her straining screams wane until whimpers replace them. Am I hurting her? Even if I am, I can't care. She wants that. She wants all of this. And she shows me as much when her hips begin to move.

"Stop, please," she begs.

I wipe the tears from her soaked cheeks. "Cry for me. I love your tears. And don't stop fighting me. It just makes it feel better when you tighten and tug on my cock."

I remind myself that she wants this as frustrated anger masks her pleasurable spasms. My fingers wind through her hair, and I yank back her head with a feral growl as I pound her pussy. "What am I?"

"My nightmare," she pants.

Mud clings to her skin as I grind her into the dirt. She whimpers from the force of each completely uninhibited movement of my hips, but I don't stop.

I almost wish I didn't have to fuck her this hard and rough, because I want to savor the feel of her warm, wet pussy squeezing me. But it's not me. It's the man I'm pretending to be to get close to her.

I'm going to come. Her walls clench around me and pump my cock with her struggles. A feral groan leaves my lips as I pin her and stall my hips, filling her tight little pussy. I twitch with every cry that racks her body. I fight the urge to make her come because I want to worship her pussy. But it's not what she asked for.

"You were a good little slut, but why were you so wet?" I ask, pinching her cheeks in my firm grasp.

"You already made me come for you," she pants.

I sure as fuck did not.

I whip my head from side to side to look around. No. He couldn't have. Could he? How would he know about our little game?

Probably the same way I knew she was in that chatroom. Sick fucking bastard.

I know I should tell her, but doing so will ruin everything for me.

For us.

"That's right," I tell her, though I know she didn't come for me.

She came for her other stalker.

Chapter Thirteen

Mariah

The sounds and smells of the coffee shop usually annoy me to no end. Not today, though. Today I feel fucking *amazing*—aside from the ache between my legs, that is. But it's a small price to pay to feel so alive. Every step reminds me of yesterday. He left some bruises on my inner thighs when he ripped my panties away, and they brush against each other every time I walk.

And I fucking love it.

It's a reminder that this really happened. I was hunted in the woods and taken against my will, which *was* my will.

I may have cried and begged for him to stop, but that was only my instinct kicking in. No matter how many times I told myself to calm down, every fiber of my being screamed that I was in danger. In a way, I really was.

The sex didn't feel super great, but all the feelings around it did. Like I was watching from above my body instead of feeling the penetration myself. The soil beneath my gripping hands. My strangled screams. The way his body looked as he so selfishly used mine. He ripped me wide open like he promised, but not just my vagina. He ripped open everything about me. He ensured the woman who left the woods was not the same woman who walked into it.

When we planned out the details in the chat, I'd told him I wanted him to leave as soon as we'd finished, but he wouldn't. He'd reached down and helped me up, and then he'd walked me back to my car without speaking. I thought it would ruin a bit of the illusion for me, but it didn't. I drove home feeling safe for the first time in days. Who knew that driving home in a puddle of come that was forced inside me would be so therapeutic?

Speaking of come, I probably shouldn't have let him fuck me raw and come inside me. Internet dating 101. But I didn't want him fumbling with a condom before he took me. I wanted it to feel as real as it could.

Mission accomplished.

Still, that choice probably wasn't my shining moment of intelligence. I'm on birth control, but it's not one hundred percent effective. What would I do if I ended up pregnant? Would I just scroll the chatroom for the mystery man? How embarrassing would that be?

My mind shifts to the first time he found me in the woods, when he made me masturbate in front of him. No matter how hard I try, I can't merge the two encounters in my mind. I didn't enjoy the first nearly as much as the second, but I can't put my finger on why. Maybe it was the knife. I was glad he didn't use it again. It wasn't part of the deal, and it nearly crossed a line for me. If he'd brought it up when we'd hashed out the details, I might have been okay with it.

"Bringing the garbage out!" I yell to the front as I gather the trash bags.

I step outside and stick the block in the path of the heavy metal door. I shuffle toward the dumpsters while wielding a heavy black bag in each hand. The hair on the back of my neck stands up and I stop and look around.

The aroma of soured milk, molding coffee grounds, and decaying food scraps turns my stomach, but something else lingers in my gut as well. A feeling, as if I'm being watched. I can't help but worry that my stalker hovers somewhere out here. Watching. Waiting. It's the same feeling that compelled me to enter the chatroom, but there's no one to fuck the fear out of me here.

"If you're going to watch me, the least you can do is help me bring out this fucking garbage!" I say.

I don't know why I'm standing here and expecting him to jump out and help me like a gentleman. All he does is lurk now. He's a passive entity with a constant presence, even when he's not there.

I scoff and push onward, making my way to the fenced area behind the shop. I lift the unwieldy metal lid and toss each bag of garbage into the dumpster's gaping mouth. One snags on the side, and ruined milk splashes onto me, coating my apron.

"Fuck."

Nothing smells quite like this, and it's not the sort of perfume I want to wear for the remainder of my shift. With a groan, I turn to go back inside, but a figure blocks my path.

Sam.

He stares at me without speaking. His hands form fists at his sides, clenching and unclenching as he continues to glare through me. My heart quickens its pace as I step back to put distance between us.

"You won't text me back," he says.

And you won't take a fucking hint, I want to say, but I don't know what state of mind he's in. There's no sense in waving a red flag in front of a bull.

"I'm sorry, Sam. I'm really not interested." I stare at the back of the building with hyper-focused vision. I need to get back inside, where it's safe. Where Sam isn't.

I try to step around him, since he's blocking the only exit out of the fenced area surrounding the dumpsters, but he doesn't move.

He licks his lips. "You may not be interested, but I am."

Now I'm annoyed enough to bite back, smart or not. "It takes two, dude."

"Not necessarily," he says, throwing his arms out and gripping the sides of the doorway.

"Does your boss know you're a creep?" I ask, raising my chin. Because honestly, fuck this guy. Olé, motherfucker.

His hand whips up to my throat, and he steps into me and backs me against the fence. It rattles behind me as my back hits the metal. "Sarah knows about everything I've done. She's my sister."

Everything he's done? So there's more? The realization that I'm not the first of his victims sends a cold chill through my limbs.

"Let go of me!"

His other hand rises to my mouth and covers it, reducing my screams to muffled whimpers. I try to become dead weight so I can get out of his hold, but the fence snags on my shirt and keeps me in place.

"Just let it happen," he groans as he grinds against me.

Fear strangles the breath from my lungs. While I set up a similar scenario with the stranger from the chatroom, there was safety in what we'd planned. There was an out. If

I ever felt uncomfortable or truly unsafe, I could have stopped everything with a single word.

Now? Now I'm trapped.

There's no trust involved in this interaction. The man in front of me cripples my entire body with panic. Instead of being simultaneously terrified and turned on, I'm only terrified. This isn't sexy. This isn't fun.

And there's nothing I can do to stop him.

Chapter Fourteen

Del

I press the button and set off my car alarm. I'm fully prepared to run over and beat the living shit out of him if this doesn't work, but he says something to her and scurries away like the vermin he is. She rushes into the building.

I was watching her until he came, and then I was watching him. I don't trust his perverted ass. When I heard her raise her voice, I knew I had to do something to get him away from her, even if it meant giving myself away. I love stalking her, but I'll give it up to protect her.

I cut off the alarm, twist the keys in the ignition, and pull away from the coffee shop. She's safe inside, and I don't want anyone to see me. This girl has terrible luck. She has two stalkers, for Christ's sake. But at least one of her stalkers is benevolent. I genuinely care about her well-being, and I don't want to hurt her. I just want to be near her.

And inside her.

The other guy has ill intentions, and I'll help her take care of him in any way I can. I'll protect her.

I park around the corner so I can ensure she gets home safely when she leaves at nine. The shop closes at seven, but she usually stays behind to clean up. I know her schedule better than my own these days.

My phone chimes.

Whorista: Are you on?

My eyes narrow on the chat. She shouldn't be doing this at work. Usually she messages me once she's home, when I can pull up her webcam and come with her. That fucking asshole must have her terrified.

ItsVenti: Yeah, I am now. What's up?
Whorista: I need a thing.
ItsVenti: What kind of thing?
Whorista: Something happened just now with my stalker.

Oh god. I hope I wasn't too late.

ItsVenti: Are you okay?
Whorista: I'm scared. And not in the way I like. I like how you scare me.

The bubbles pop up and down at the bottom of the screen for far too long. She's indecisive about what she wants to say, but she doesn't need to be. I know what she wants, and I'm more than happy to provide it.

Finally, she musters the courage.

Whorista: I need the fear fucked out of me.

ItsVenti: Where are you?

I ask this question, but I know exactly where she is. I always know where she is these days.

Whorista: The coffee shop on the strip, with the big cappuccino painting in the window. We're closing soon, but I'm last on shift tonight.

ItsVenti: I know exactly where it is. I'll be there soon. Leave the door unlocked for me.

I wait in the car for a few minutes because it can't look like I'm sitting right around the fucking corner, waiting for her. The silence gives me too much time to think.

Something has to be done about Sam. He's gotta go, but I'm not a killer. Though I may get to that point if he hurts her.

Maybe it doesn't have to get to that point.

If I could slip into the house and lace his eye drops with something that will blind him, he can't look at my venti girl anymore. He can't creep on young girls anymore, either. He won't be able to torment anyone ever again. I take a few more minutes to play around with my idea before starting my car and heading toward the café.

I park, pull my mask from the back seat, and situate it over my face. The front door has been left unlocked. Good girl. As I enter the dark café, a feeling of unease weaves through the air. The silence unnerves me a bit. The machines that usually whir and hum all day lie dormant, and the absence of the low hum of quiet conversation only adds to the eerie mood. I want to call out for her, but that would ruin the fun.

I skulk toward the back room, purse my lips, and let out

a high-pitched whistle. "Hide, hide, little whore. Because when I catch you . . . I'll fuck you."

I peer over and under metal racks in search of her. When I open cabinets, I search inside. I turn around and her discarded apron lies on the floor. It wasn't there before. Which means she *is* here.

But where?

I peer behind supply boxes holding different types of coffees and cups. A maze of cardboard. But then I see the metal door. Would she hide there, waiting for her nightmare to haunt her?

I whip open the door, and cool air rushes around me before I even step inside. She's hidden inside a walk-in cooler, but I can warm her up.

"Little whore? Come out for your nightmare! Let me see you."

Cups, lids, and a metric fuck ton of coffee line the walls. I step further inside and find her curled up on the floor beside a rack, trying to hide from me. She screams when she sees me. I grab her by the hair and pull her to her feet. My hand roves down her body, and she shivers against me.

"How'd you find me?" she asks, a tremble in her voice.

"Because you aren't very smart, whore," I growl. Why she ran into such a cold part of this old building is beyond me. "Your body is so fucking tight from the cold. I wonder how cool you'll feel from the inside."

"I don't want that," she whispers, but there's a fire in her eyes this time that makes me certain she does. She's so fucking horny for me, even if she wants to play the part of the helpless victim.

"I bet you do. If I put my hand down your pants, I'll find a soaking-wet pussy, huh?"

She shakes her head, so I prove her wrong. I pull her

closer and slide my hand down her pants. Her warm wetness feels like boiling heat compared to the cool air around us.

"How can I force you when your pussy is so welcoming, whore?"

I reach around me and grab a knife from the shelf behind her. We agreed on no weapons the first time we met, but she has an out if she's uncomfortable with this. I wait to make sure she's okay with the change in plans before I continue. When she doesn't say the word to stop me, I press the blade against her cheek and ease it down her skin with minimal pressure. She closes her eyes.

What trust she has in a stranger.

I bring the knife lower and cut her shirt. When the blade grazes her stomach, she whimpers. I pull the ragged fabric from her body, exposing her round tits. Peaked nipples strain toward me from those perfect mounds.

I run the blade over the sensitive skin before bringing it to her throat. She cries out as I push her against the rack, turn her around, and lean her forward. Her chest grazes the cool metal. With the knife firmly planted against her throat, I use my other hand to lower her slacks. The skin beneath her clothes is warm. I wasn't sure I could perform in such a chilly room, but the moment her ass and pussy are exposed to me, I harden like those fucking nipples of hers.

"No," she pants. "Please, nightmare."

"Please what?"

She should tell me to stop, but she doesn't. She wants me. Her dripping pussy screams for me to keep going, even if she can't.

My hand seeks out her warmth, and I push my fingers inside her. She gasps as I sink up to my knuckles. I pull back and slip another finger inside her, stretching her.

Every time I pull out of her, the chill melds with my wet fingers. I hope she feels that icy blast when I sink inside her again.

I finger-fuck her until her screams change, filling with feral pleasure as I hit such a sensitive spot inside her. I pull my fingers from her just in time for a gush of her come to follow. She squirts all over the floor. How unhygienic.

I love it.

If it were colder in here, her come would become slick ice on the floor. Instead, it squirts all over her employer's supplies. I keep making her gush, over and over, until she's breathless and panting.

"No more, please," she begs.

"You will give me however many orgasms I want to take from you," I growl, assaulting her pussy again.

She screams out, leaning forward to escape my touch as she puts weight into the knife at her throat. I pull out and let her spray the floor again, knowing the remnants of this evening will be there for her boss to find tomorrow. I won't allow her to clean it up.

"Stop!" she screams.

I pull out of her wet, red, swollen pussy for the last time and give her body a reprieve.

"You want your nightmare to fuck you, don't you?" I whisper in her ear.

She shakes her head.

"Too fucking bad. You're mine to do with as I please. Mine to use. Mine to fill."

I throw the knife aside and go for my belt. I snatch it through the loops, eager to free myself, then I put it around her neck, put it through the buckle, and let it tighten. Her hands instinctively go for her throat to grip the leather between panicked fingers. I hold it like a leash as I crane her neck and push her further into the metal rack with the weight of my body.

My cock rests against her slit. I draw my hips back and push inside her. My piercing snags on her opening, and a different sound rushes from her lips. My aim isn't to hurt her, but I keep pushing. It'll feel good once it's inside her.

She moans, unable to stay in character as I thrust. Temperature play at its natural finest. The warm heat of skin when everything around you is an icy wonderland. Friction warms us further as I fuck her. I squeeze the belt, and her moans take on a dizzying undertone. I'm sure that blood choke is making her warm and fuzzy too. Just one more play on the temperature.

I fuck her, thrusting deep and then shallow so I can feel the cold along my length before I sink into her again. My hand rises to her chest, and I take her full breast into my palm and squeeze. She groans and pushes her ass against me. Her hands grip the rack as I fuck her harder, faster, until she can't control the glorious sounds erupting from her mouth. The rack rattles from the force of each thrust, and I worry everything on top of it will come crashing down.

But I don't stop. I just keep pounding into her.

"Beg your nightmare for his come," I growl.

"I want it," she pants.

"Beg me, slut."

"Give me your come," she pleads, her voice rising.

"Good little whore. You're such a greedy girl."

And I give it to her. Every drop. I hope she can feel the burn of it inside her.

I pull out of her and paint her ass with the rest of it. It'll cool so quickly against her skin. My hand goes to her ear, and I rub the sensitive lobe before releasing the belt around her throat.

Her body tenses. She straightens her back, turns, and stares at me. Her mouth gapes open. "Del?"

My heart literally fucking stops, then crashes against the wall of my chest and dies again.

"No . . ." I say, but her hands go for my mask before I can say anything else. I try to stop her, but she pulls it off before I can move. "Let me explain!"

"Pumpkin!" she screams before sending a knee into my nuts.

I fall to my knees and land in the chilly slick of her come. I grip the metal rack in front of me and inhale sharp breaths as the pain radiates from my groin to my stomach. She races from the cooler, and I worry she'll lock me inside on her way out, but she's too panicked and frazzled to think of that.

Thank god.

"Mariah!" I scream.

I want her to stop and hear me out. I didn't mean to touch her like that. I was lost in the memory of how it made her feel at the photo shoot. A slave to the moment, I only wanted to bring her a little more pleasure. Now my weakness has ripped the veil away and ruined our arrangement.

I drag myself to my feet and limp out of the back room. Her apron no longer lies on the floor. She's gone.

Well, fuck. It's over, and I'll never see her again. And I can't handle that thought. I need her more than I need the air in my lungs or the blood pumping through my fucking veins. If I don't have her, I have nothing.

I have to win her back.

Chapter Fifteen

Mariah

Fuck that guy. I mean, who does he think he is? How'd he even find me in the chatroom? Is he stalking me too? How does so much horrific shit even happen to one person? How do I meet two people that fuck up my night so colossally that I'm wearing a stained apron as a shirt as I drive home in the middle of the fucking night?

And to top it all off, I'm full of his come.

I pull into my driveway and rush inside before anyone sees me, because this is the biggest walk of shame in history. The moment I get inside, I rush to the bathroom, strip off my apron, and begin cleaning the mess between my legs. I want to scream. I want to cry. But I do neither. I go to the fetish website, block the fucking chatroom, and delete the stupid app off my phone. I'm done with it all.

Fucking men.

Fucking stalkers.

Oh, yeah. My stalker! Well, Sam, since I have to clarify who is who because I have *two* of them. I haven't even given myself a moment to process what happened at the dumpster. He's getting braver.

This is fucking insane.

This is all my fault.

This is what happens when you let fear turn into something else inside you.

I've done stupid shit like go into some online chat room looking for some strange. Because realistically, what were my chances of finding someone normal to fulfill some new fantasy my vagina conjured up because she got a little scared?

Alone in my house, I no longer feel safe. There aren't enough locks on the doors and windows. I feel as if everyone is coming for me now. As if my world is so much smaller all of a sudden.

I can't give these fucking men the power to make me feel so small and scared. They don't deserve that. I have to find a way to take back my life. My sanity.

This is such a goddamn mess, and I wish I'd never gone to that photo shoot.

Del

Even several days later, I can't stop thinking about her. Especially here, just outside Sarah's house. At the place it all began. Flashes of our shoot cross my mind. I pull the picture from my pocket and run my thumb across the glossy surface.

We looked happy. We looked like we could have been

something more. Then I had to go and fuck it up. Her face in the picture is so different from the look on her face in the cooler when she realized I'd do anything to be with her, even if it meant being someone else.

Sirens wail in the distance. This is the only house on the road, so I'm certain they're heading here. I'm hidden in the brush, but I fall back a bit more to ensure I won't be spotted. I squat behind a bush and watch the house. Faint screaming continues inside, and a smirk draws my lips upward because I know the source of each pained wail.

It's perfect.

If I can't be with Mariah, if I can't protect her, I've at least gotten rid of the bigger problem.

The ambulance pulls up the driveway. Uniformed men take their time going inside, but the screaming finally stops. They haul him outside on a stretcher, and thick gauze pads cover each eye. They can't hide the reddening skin around the white squares, though.

I hope he's blind.

I hope his eyes never see Mariah again.

Sarah steps onto the porch. A tissue rests in her hands, and she uses it to dab her eyes. She shouldn't cry over him. He's a pervert. She watches as the ambulance drives him away.

I initially considered planting some pictures on his computer and reporting him to the police, but perpetual darkness is worse for someone like him. He can no longer look at unsuspecting women and young girls.

I'm comfortable with my decision.

As I make my way through the woods, a heaviness hangs over me. I thought getting rid of Sam would help me feel better, but it doesn't. My thoughts still circle Mariah in a never-ending loop. She consumes my every waking thought. She sucks the soul from me in every dream.

During the day, visions of our trysts haunt me. Chasing her through the woods. Having sex with her. The way she couldn't stay in character in the cooler because she wanted me that badly. Those memories are ingrained in my brain.

I would do anything to take back that moment in the cooler. How far could we have gone if I hadn't touched her earlobe? Was she an orgasm away from falling in love with me? Would our conversations have switched from pure sex to something more? I could have remained her nightmare, but I could have been her dream too.

When I reach my car, I make a decision. I'm going to confront her. Because why not? What do I have to lose? She's gone off the chat. User not found. If I text her, she'll just block my number. I need to come face to face with her. I need to explain myself at least. She can deny me all she wants after that, but I at least need a chance to explain why I did what I did.

So I turn the keys in the ignition and drive toward the coffee shop like any normal, sane human would do. I park outside and head into the building, where I meld into the back of a line that nearly snakes out the door.

I spot her behind the counter. Her dark hair bobs in a ponytail as she rushes from one machine to the other. She hasn't seen me, and watching her in her element is almost too much to bear. She bites her lip to avoid saying something to a rude customer. She brushes her hair back when she's flustered. She's so focused on everything in front of her, and I can't help but wonder when she'll notice me or how her face will change when she finally does.

The line gets shorter. Now there's only a handful of angry, bitter customers who need their coffee just to keep from killing themselves or the people around them. I'm still a ghost in line. A quiet, unrelenting spirit haunting the coffee shop where she works.

Finally, I'm in the front of the line. But her coworker waits on me.

"A large coffee, black."

She looks at me as if I'm a maniac for waiting in line for something I could easily prepare at home, but the coffee isn't what I'm here for. Where is Mariah? She ran into the back a few minutes ago, but I figured she'd be at the counter by now.

I pay the woman and turn to leave, but I didn't wait in line for forty-five minutes to drive home without speaking to her. I wait until her coworker busies herself with the next person in line, and then I slip behind the counter.

Sneaking into the back is easy enough. I should have just done this in the first place. I find her bent over a box, digging through an assortment of cups inside. One tumbles over the side, rolls toward me, and hits my foot. I pick it up and hold it toward her.

"It's a venti," I say. A play on my username in the chat.

Mariah drops the cups in her hands and freezes. She doesn't get up or move. She just stays squatted down in front of the box, as if refusing to acknowledge me means I'll go away.

I'm not going anywhere.

"Can we talk?" I ask.

She wipes a tear from her cheek and stands up. She doesn't look at me as she scoops the cups from the floor and tries to walk past me. I grab her arm.

"I need to bring these up front. They're waiting for me." She rips away from me.

"I'm not letting you leave until we talk."

"Get the fuck out of my way, Del, or I'll—"

"You'll what?"

A frustrated breath blows her hair away from her forehead.

"Mariah, where are the cups?" her coworker yells from the front. "The crowd's getting impatient!"

"I have to go, Del," she says, her eyes narrowing on mine.

I put my arm out to keep her from moving away. "Give me five fucking minutes, Mariah. Please."

"You have two minutes."

I'll take it.

"I'm sorry I hid who I was, but what we had was real. *Is* real. No matter who was beneath the mask, me or your nightmare, that man would do absolutely anything to be with you."

She swallows. "You lied to me. You're the one who ran off from the shoot like I disgusted you. Why do all this to be with someone you couldn't stand to be around a second longer than you had to?"

"I had to leave because I couldn't handle knowing that once I left, I'd never see you again. I thought it would be better to sever it that way than to say a goodbye that would break me. I'm sorry for running away like that." I brush her hair away from her flushed cheeks. "But I'm not sorry for everything that happened after that. Part of it was a selfish need to see you again, but I also had to keep you safe from your stalker."

"Stalk*ers*," she clips. "Plural."

"You don't know what he's capable of. He's out to hurt you. I only wanted to be near you."

"That's not an excuse, Del."

She's right. It's not. "I'm sorry."

A shrill voice cuts through the air. *"The cups, Mariah!"*

"I'm fucking coming!" She closes her eyes, then looks at me with a softening glare. "Come to my house tonight. I'm sure you know where it is." Then she ducks beneath my arm, and she's gone as if she was never there at all.

Chapter Sixteen

Mariah

I can't believe I told Del he could come by my house after work. I wish I didn't have anything more to say to him and that I could just put him in the past, but he's so fucking convincing when he's standing right in front of me. Which I'm sure was his intention. Surely it can't hurt to hear him out, though.

Right?

"Can I have a medium coffee?" The familiar voice halts my thoughts. I don't want to hear it, especially when I'm already dealing with a metric fuck ton of confusion. Maybe I'm just imagining things. After what happened last night, I'm on edge.

I turn around as slowly as I can. I've almost convinced myself that I'm hearing things, that I'll see a stranger at the counter, but my mouth drops open when I meet his eyes.

Or the space where his eyes should be, I guess.

It's Sam, one of my two stalkers. Red, raw tissue rims the dark sunglasses on his face, but when the light catches just right, I can see a hint of the swollen mess behind the shades. I take a few steps to the left, then the right, but his head doesn't turn to follow my movements.

"Is Mariah here?" he asks.

I'm right in front of him. But he can't see me.

My coworker looks back at me, and I shake my head furiously. I don't want him to know I'm here.

"She just left a little while ago," she says.

Sam taps the counter with a cane and lets a curse loose under his breath. "Can you give her this?" He slides a picture toward my coworker, and she picks it up.

Her lips tighten. "Sure."

He turns around and leaves before even getting his coffee.

"Sir, what about your order?" she asks.

"Forget it," he says, waving her off as he leaves.

She turns toward me and slides the picture across my palm with a disgusted scoff. I look at the image and nearly choke on my spit. It's a picture of me rubbing myself in the woods. Which can only mean . . .

"I have to go," I say without looking back at my coworker.

"Probably best," she says.

Now he's not only ruined my personal life, he's ruined my public life as well. How can I show my face around here when everyone will know my dirty little secret by the next shift change?

I remove my apron and rush out the back door, hoping to avoid Sam despite all the burning questions now roasting my organs.

The doorbell rings. How cute that my stalker would announce himself this way. I go to the door and throw the picture in Del's face the moment he steps across the threshold into my home.

"What's—" When he holds the picture out, he realizes what exactly it is.

"Why did he have that?" I ask. I try to keep my voice from shaking, but it's useless.

"Mariah, I can—"

"Were you two working together? Was this all some sick fucking game you guys decided to play with me?"

He shakes his head. "No. I didn't know he was in the woods that night until you said I made you come before I caught you."

"Bullshit!"

"I swear to god, Mariah. That's why I walked you to your fucking car when we were done. I didn't want him to hurt you."

"How nice of you. What a gentleman!" I don't know what I believe anymore.

"When I found out he was stalking you . . ." He shakes his head.

I take a deep breath. "Have I ever slept with him?"

"It was me in the woods and the cooler. If there were any other times, I'll take more than just his vision from him."

The relief I feel at hearing this is short-lived because even though it's always been him, fuck him for doing this to me in the first place. And then the rest of his sentence sits on my chest.

"So you did that to him?"

"For you."

"You can't say that was for me, Del. I didn't ask you to do that!"

"I had to protect you."

I sigh. I want to hate him for that admission, but I can't. I'm torn between feelings of disgust and pride. On one hand, he's proven what he's capable of. On the other, he's proven he'll do anything to keep me safe.

He grips my arm and pulls me into him. "I'm sorry for what I've done to keep you safe, but I'm not sorry for protecting you. I'll do whatever it takes to protect you, I promise you that. Just let me catch you again, Mariah."

"Del . . ."

"No. I inhale your scent with every breath I take. You live rent free inside me." He lifts his shirt, exposing a beautiful tattoo of a fall tree. A camera sits on the bench beneath the tree.

I gasp and look back toward my bedroom as I pull away from him and rush to grab the sketchbook from my desk. I flip to the page and confirm it's the picture I drew after the photo shoot. Once again, flattery and frustration fight for dominance in my mind.

I stomp back to the living room and push the sketchbook toward him. "Was this supposed to woo me? This means you've been in my house without my permission."

"I'm sorry, Mariah. It's just such a good drawing, and it proves that day affected you too."

My cheeks flush. No one has ever been so simultaneously offensive and sweet. It's causing a mixed reaction in my gut, and I don't know what to do with it. Seeing my drawing off paper is a dream come true. I just didn't expect it to be on my stalker's body. One of my stalkers, that is.

"I hate you for what you did." I study my feet before allowing my gaze to rise to his. "But I love you for thinking my silly art was good enough to put on your body."

"It's not silly art."

I step toward him, allowing myself to get closer in so many ways. It feels like I'm standing near the edge of a cliff. If I take a few steps forward, I could see a beautiful view. But I'm also taking a risk. "How do I know the rest of those times were you?"

"Do you need me to remind you of how my piercing felt when it raked your pussy?"

I forgot about the pretty black barbells beneath his cock. It was hard to focus on them when I was being chased and forced because that sort of experience made me feel everything at once. But I definitely felt them in the cooler before I got so upset that I let it slip my memory once again. And he's right. The man who took me in the woods and in the cooler had the same black barbells.

"Maybe you need to feel it at the back of your throat to jog your memory?" he asks. I'm close enough that his warm breath caresses the top of my head.

My heart catches in my throat. He's so crass compared to the man I remember at the shoot. Is this what I draw out of him? What he draws out of me? He pissed me off and I've been mad at him, but I've also given myself to him, even if I didn't know it was him. He had all of me in the palm of his hand, and I miss that.

I miss *him*.

"Yes, I want you to remind me," I whimper.

His hands land on my shoulders and push me onto my knees. I come face to face with my drawing as he lifts the hem of his shirt to undo his jeans. I scrutinize it at this level. I wish I'd cleaned up the line work, but how was I supposed to know it would end up immortalized on his body?

His fingers wind through my hair, then he squeezes, sending a bolt of pleasurable pain through my scalp. "Taste your nightmare, venti."

His nickname for me warms me. My nickname for him sets me on fire.

"My nightmare," I repeat before he shoves his cock past my lips.

His dick feels familiar in my mouth, as if I could point it out in a crowd by feeling it inside me, even if I never saw his face. It's him. The man I've given myself to. The man I've allowed to chase and hunt me. He's embraced my misaligned kink and let me live it out through him. This cock is safety, even if he's done some fucked-up things.

My nose taps my artwork as my head bobs lower, and I realize how amazing the art from my hand looks on his body. I'm connected to my muse in a mind-bending way, and I'll never get my thoughts straightened out after this. His body is suddenly my mural, and I want to drip my pleasure onto it.

He holds my head still and takes control, and I gag on his cock as he fucks my throat. The piercing brushes the sensitive skin just past the back of my tongue. My eyes water, but I don't stop him. I want him to use me.

He pulls his cock from my mouth and lifts me to my feet, and his hand wipes away the drool collecting on my chin.

"I want you inside me, nightmare," I whisper as he cranes my neck and examines me.

"You want the man who stalked and hunted you inside your pretty little pussy?"

I bite my tongue and nod against his grasp.

"What you want has always been my command, venti." He kisses me, and all of that fiery possession pours into my mouth as his lips spread on mine. He's sucking my soul from my body with nothing more than his kiss.

He drags me toward my room, and I push down the nip of discomfort when he knows right where it is. He lays me down on the bed and goes to the bathroom. When he returns, he holds the bottle of moisturizer in his hand. I want to ask what it's for, but then he begins to strip me and words escape my brain. Once I'm naked before him, he puts a bit of the moisturizer into his hand and rubs it into my cheeks, moving out until he's reached my earlobes. I close my eyes and let out a breathy moan.

"Do you recognize that scent?" he asks as his fingertips massage my earlobes and send pleasure radiating through me.

"Strawberries," I tell him.

"And?"

My closed eyes whip open. "And what?"

"Think about it. How does it smell as you've rubbed it on your perfect face every single day?"

My mind swirls. It has had a unique tinge of a scent, but do I even want to know? "What did you do to my lotion?"

His eyebrow rises, and a smirk crosses his face. "You've been rubbing me on you too."

Rubbing him on me? What does he—Oh god. "Please tell me you did *not* come in my lotion!"

"Oh, I did. I wanted to be on you even when I couldn't touch you. I wanted every single person who inhales that scent to smell me too."

I push him away. "Del, I can't believe you did that!"

"But you must like how I smell or you wouldn't have kept wearing it."

I did like how he smelled. I just didn't know it was him. "What else did you do in my room? Did you touch me while I was sleeping?"

I will stab him with the pencil on the nightstand if he did.

"No, venti. As much as I wanted to, I wouldn't do that to you. But when I saw you lying there, I *needed* to come, and if I couldn't touch you, I had to touch myself."

"You didn't need to touch yourself over my fucking lotion bottle!"

"Oh, I did. It was either that or my come was going on your body. I was being respectful," he says.

"Respectful my ass," I clip.

"Why do I feel like you wish I'd touched you while you slept?"

My breath catches in my throat. Is that why I'm more upset about where he came than the fact that he came at all? Jesus Christ, no. Why do all these situations warp into something that turns me on? I should be running to call the police, not leaping onto his dick.

"Tomorrow night," he says, "why don't you take some sleeping pills and go to bed for me? We'll see what happens."

"And tonight?"

He spreads my legs before grabbing my hips and dragging me to the edge of the bed. He breathes warm air on my slit. "Tonight, I'll eat your pussy the way I've wanted to since the day I met you."

His tongue slips from his mouth and brushes against my clit. I whimper and drop my head to the mattress. Two of his fingers push inside me as he lashes me with his tongue and fuck, it feels good. No one has eaten me the way he is right now. Like I'm a buffet laid out in front of him.

He sucks and nibbles my clit before going back to those quick, broad licks. I moan into the air, my body curling against my will as my muscles tense and tighten with every stroke of his tongue or piston of his fingers inside me.

I push against him, burying his face in my pussy. He grips my hips and embraces the tight seal my lips have created around his. He groans and growls into my flesh, and I realize that he's pulled his hands from me so that he can jerk himself off.

The thought of him stroking himself as his mouth works me brings me so fucking close. I grind against his face as he leads me toward my edge. Then he changes his motions, and it's enough to send a barrage of lights flashing behind my closed lids. I come on his face. Hard.

He pulls off his shirt and his hand leaves my hip to fuck me with his fingers as he impales me with three of them. An intense pleasure builds in my gut. He pulls out just in time to make me come with an intense feeling, and I squirt all over his bare chest.

"Fuck, that's a good girl. Come again for me, venti. I want you to soak me with it."

He puts his fingers back inside me and fucks me harder and faster until that unbearable pressure barrels down on me. He pulls out and I squirt all over him again. The sound of splashing liquid fights with his feral groans as I cover him in my come.

"Del," I pant.

He lies down beside me and motions to the glistening mess on his chest. "Come clean it off me."

Before I can move, he grips my hair and drags me closer. I open my mouth and press my tongue to his hot flesh, lapping up the salty-sweet come he drew from me. He strokes himself as my tongue flickers across his chest and down his abdomen, paying particular attention to that tattoo beside his hip. He groans as his strokes increase in tempo, and I consider hopping on him and riding him. Before I can, he lets out a low groan.

"I'm coming," he growls. White beads spill from the head of his cock. It spurts out and lands on his lower stomach, and a final bead lands on the tattoo. I go for it with my tongue, cleaning off the little bench now stained with his pleasure.

Now that we're both satisfied, a sadness creeps into my gut. I want to ask him to stay, but it feels too soon for that. So I settle on the next best thing.

"Will I see you again tomorrow, nightmare?" I ask.

He stands up and grabs his shirt from the floor. "Right now, I'm not your nightmare, but tomorrow night, I will be."

I can't wait.

Chapter Seventeen

Del

Snowflakes drift from the sky as I stand outside her house the next night. The streetlights catch the delicate ice crystals and allow them to shine. The temperature has dropped, and it feels like we lost twenty degrees in the last twenty-four hours. Despite the cold, my body is a furnace because I'm thinking about her.

Before I left her house last night, she told me to play with her, even if she doesn't wake up. She wants me to keep going no matter what. It makes me nervous because if she's asleep, how will I know if I go too far? But she made me promise I wouldn't stop. She wants to feel me when I'm long gone in the morning. She wants to know I was inside her when she wakes up. That's what she told me, and I'll happily oblige her newfound fantasy.

I creep across the lawn and sneak in through a window in the back of the house. I didn't want her to leave any doors unlocked with Sam still around. Even if he can't see, he's still a threat. His blindness is a mere stumbling block, but men like him will find a way around it if given enough time to adjust.

My sneakers hit the ground, and I let myself drop from the windowsill into her kitchen. I head toward her room. The night light illuminates her bedside and casts a pale glow across her face. She looks beautiful when she sleeps.

I rub my hand down her arm, but she doesn't stir. When I pull back the blanket, she continues to sleep. Her breathing remains slow and even. I move her onto her back and her arm flops off the bed. I lift it and set it beside her, then I raise the hem of her shirt and rub my hand along her lower belly. So soft and warm. I lean down and kiss the skin, then give it a little nip. She still doesn't move.

I don't know if she drugged herself or if she's faking, but if it's all pretend, she's fucking good at it.

The fabric rises higher, and her tits fall from beneath it. I lean over, take the hard peak into my mouth, and suck. Then I bite with enough pressure to wake her, but she doesn't move. She's not faking it.

I caress and rub the curves of her chest, thrumming her nipples with my thumb. Her panties grow wet for me, and I tug them off. Her pussy gleams with a slick shine that reflects the light. I spread her lips with my fingers and rub her clit, but then I remember she's asleep. She isn't aware of this. I don't need to satisfy her. Her body is mine to use as selfishly as I please, and I don't have to think about making her come. Though I know I'll still think of it. All the beautiful sounds she makes and the way her pleasure coats me.

But tonight she wants me to use her, so I'll give my venti what she wants.

I climb onto her bed and drop between her thighs, then I lean down and kiss her. With our current arrangement, I haven't had enough chances to press my lips against hers. I wish she didn't have such kissable fucking lips.

I sit up, hook her thighs over mine, and pull down my sweatpants. My cock falls from the fabric and rests against her. Her head is turned to the side. I lean back and spit on her pussy, and though my warm saliva drips down to coat us both, there's still tight friction as I draw my hips back and push inside her.

Silence greets my intrusion, and I miss that whimper she makes when I first ease into her.

I thrust forward, making her take me deep inside her. To my pleasure, she stirs a bit, a confused moan leaving her lips. She probably thinks she's dreaming. I hope her wet dream involves me stretching her from the inside out.

I revel in her warmth and fuck her until her distant moans grow closer to the surface of consciousness. When I pull out of her, it's just to flip her onto her belly. Her body is dead weight as I turn her over.

I sandwich her against the mattress and put myself back inside her. I bury my face into her long black hair as I thrust. She smells so good, but the best part? She smells like the lotion I tainted. I smell it on her neck and face.

I always want her coated in me.

She drifts off again as I fuck her. I increase the speed and pressure until painful pleasure wakes her up once more. She moans softly.

"Nightmare?" she whispers.

"It's okay, venti. Sleep while I use you. You wanted me to enjoy your body all night long, to fuck and fill you over and over so that you wake up sore and missing my cock, so that's what I'm giving you. You'll wake up a come-filled mess. Dirty and full. All for your nightmare."

"Yes," she whispers with a tired heaviness in her voice. "Please."

"Good girl. Sleeping fucking beauty."

I bury my hand in her hair and fuck her harder and faster so that she'll feel every memory of each thrust with every step she takes in the morning. I'll leave an imprint of this night inside her.

My hand drops to her hip so I can get a better grip and press against her ass as I bury myself deeper inside her. I bottom out, and my thrusts grow shallow. Pleasure drags a nail up my spine.

Thoughts of her waking up filled with my come make my balls tighten. These visions light my brain on fire. I want my come to drip from her and spread all over her soft, velvet thighs. She'll need to take a shower to clean off the sheer volume of my pleasure when she gets up.

God. She's incredible. And she deserves every drop I have to give.

I thrust one final time to the back of her pussy, and I bust. I fill her with all that I've been saving for her. All that she asked for.

When I have nothing left to give, I lie beside her. My cock glistens as I rest it against her ass and pull her into me. I put her limp leg over mine and put my fingers between her legs. I'm not trying to get her off—she's still asleep—but I don't want to waste my come. As it drips from her, I catch it, swirl it, and push it back inside her, ensuring she's a mess.

Because of me.

I keep my fingers stuffed inside her. First one, then two. I want to hold it inside until I'm hard enough to pull out of her and use her again. One load isn't enough. She needs all of me.

I lean over and kiss her loose lips. "We're going to have such a good night, venti."

The night is just beginning, after all. I plan to fuck her until there's nothing more to give her when I come. When I've given her my absolute all.

Because I want to give her everything.

Chapter Eighteen

Del

I spent the night fucking her. Once turned to twice, then three times. By the time the sun peeked through the curtain, I think I'd filled her four or five times. I lost count. And then, against my own wishes, I left her wrapped in her sheets and filled with loads of my come. It's what she wanted.

I've been lying on my bed for hours now, unable to sleep. I can't stop thinking about her and how she must have felt when she woke up. Has she showered and washed me away yet? Or did she head off to work with our combined mess between her legs?

Fuck.

I look at my phone and check the tracker I installed on her cell. It says she's still at home. Weird. It's Thursday, and she works mornings. Maybe she overslept or she's too hungover from the meds.

Or what if she took too much of the drugs?

My chest tightens at the thought of something bad

happening to her. Just to make sure she didn't leave her phone at home, I call into her job. I get a curt greeting from the other end.

"Hello, is Mariah working today?"

"No, she never showed up," the woman says, sounding really flustered and busy.

Panic clenches my gut as I hang up. Running on autopilot, I get into my car and rush over to her house. The fear that she overdosed remains in the front of my mind. I shouldn't have left her alone. She was waking up by the end of my night with her, and I thought she'd be okay. Oh god, this is all my fault.

Her front door is still locked, just how I left it, and her car is still in the driveway. The prospect of finding her dead in the bed fills me with an indescribable fear. I climb through the window again and nearly fall onto my ass because my sweat-coated palms are too slippery. I rush to the bedroom, and what I find strangles the air from my lungs.

She's not in the bed, but a large red stain is.

I drop to my knees and my face comes within inches of the red stain on the tan sheet. The splatter drags from where I left her to the edge.

Oh god, where is she?

I stand up and look around. I don't know what to do or how to find her, but I'm certain Sam is somehow behind all of this.

I drop her phone onto the nightstand and rush back out the door. I don't even bother locking it. When I get into my car, I blindly drive to the familiar house in the woods. Would he have her at their house? Doubtful, but it's the only lead I have.

No one appears to be home as I sneak back inside the

isolated house where this all started. I dig around the office again. Instead of looking for Mariah's information, I'm looking for something that will tell me where Sarah's nitwit brother would have taken my girl. There's paperwork about his parole stuffed in a drawer. In another, I find a book of deposit slips for checks. There's a photo lab that has deposits every month. Are they renting this place?

There's only one way to find out.

Mariah

Cloth restraints bind my wrists together behind my back. Itchy, dried blood cakes my temple. I look around and blink to adjust to the darkness. Pictures line the room. Pictures of me and Del, but Del's face has been scratched out in each image.

Fucking Sam.

He came into my room this morning, startling me awake despite my heavy, drug-induced haze. I still tried to fight him off, but then he hit me with something, and I woke up here. In this room.

"Help!" I scream. "Can anyone hear me?"

My question goes unanswered, which may be a good thing. The only person who would respond is the person who put me here in the first place.

I jerk my body, and the chair squeals along the floor as I try to get out of the restraints. Both of my legs have been secured to the chair. Everything is immobile. For being blind, he sure can tie a person up.

"Hello, Mariah," Sam says as he walks into the room.

Light outlines his form, casting him in deep shadows. That means it's daylight outside. Would anyone even know I'm missing? My coworker probably hates me and thinks I overslept or something. It wouldn't be the first time.

"Sam, you have to let me go," I say, raising my chest with feigned confidence.

He laughs. "That's not going to happen."

"Why are you doing this?"

"All you had to do was let me love you and it wouldn't have come to this."

"You don't love me. You don't even know me!"

Sam turns away from me and steps toward the pictures. His fingers graze an image before he rips it down and stares at it.

He stares at it?

"You can see that?" I ask.

"Yes, and I also saw you telling your coworker to tell me you weren't there."

I swallow. "I thought you were blind . . ."

"Your little boyfriend blinded my left eye, but I didn't put as much in the right eye because it had started burning by the time the drops hit my skin. I have most of my vision in that eye."

"I'm sorry, Sam. I didn't mean anything by it," I say. I absolutely did, but I need to lie to him. I have to make it out of here somehow.

He looks at the picture in his hand again. "Why him and not me?"

I don't even know how to answer that. What happened with Sam was only at the command of his sister, but he clearly felt something I can't reciprocate.

"Del and I—"

"He's better looking than me, isn't he? He's not scarred." He points toward the gnarly marks around his eyes and down his cheeks.

No, he's not a psycho.

But he kind of is, just not in the same way. I can find safety in our most dangerous moments. With Sam, it's just fear and an uneasy feeling.

When I don't answer, he reaches for a camera on the desk and snaps a picture of me. The huge bulb causes a blinding rush of color to block my vision. The camera shutter clicks again, and I wince from the bright light.

"So beautiful," he whispers. His thumb caresses the backlit screen. He places the camera on the table and turns to me. "Now I want to get some more risqué shots. Are you ready to be my perfect model?"

I shake my head. If the choice lies between death and being subjected to his non-consensual fetishes, I'd rather die. There is no safe word with Sam.

A door slams somewhere in the house, and our heads snap toward the sound.

"What the fuck?" he growls as he takes a step toward the door. Before he makes it much further, the door whips open and the daylight shines through again. I'm still half-blind from the camera's flash, so I can't make out any of this person's features, but a familiar voice sends my hope sailing skyward.

"What the fuck do you think you're doing with her?" Del asks.

"How'd you find me?" Sam's voice is almost a whimper.

"You're not the only stalker in the room. Just like when you followed her into the woods, huh? That's your simple MO?"

Del rushes forward, but Sam snatches up the camera

and flashes the bright bulb of light at Del. It stops him in his path. His hands move to cover his eyes, but it's too late.

"How does it feel to be blind, Del?" Sam asks. He waits until Del tries to open his eyes again before flashing the camera once more.

"Fuck!" Del screams.

"Seems more fair this way, doesn't it? For you to be as blind as me?" His voice has shifted from a whimper to a shrill caw of excitement. It's like nails on a fucking chalkboard.

"I'm going to kill you!" Del yells, feeling across the table behind him as he follows Sam's voice.

I cry out as the sounds of flesh hitting flesh break through the silence. I don't know who's hitting who. Something crashes against the floor and breaks, and someone grunts as the air is knocked out of their lungs. I want to rub my eyes and get this terrible glare to go away so that I can see, but the ties around my wrists refuse to budge.

When the flickering orbs in my eyes wane and I can finally see, I wish I was still blind. Sam straddles Del, sending a fist into his face over and over. If he loses, then I lose too. What will Sam do with me? Kill me? Keep me as his fucking pet?

"Come on, Del!" I scream. "You're better than him!"

My encouragement seems to help, and he lifts his hip and flips Sam onto his back. The roles reverse and the pounding continues, only this time I'm overjoyed by every thud I hear.

"You ruined my life!" Sam growls.

"You're a pedo, you creepy fuck!" Del sends his fist into Sam's nose. "You ruined your own life!"

Could that be true? How would he know? At this point, it doesn't surprise me. I fight harder against my restraints. If he has a history of hurting people—and children, at that—there's no telling what he's willing to do.

"You didn't need to blind me!" Sam yells.

"I didn't want your eyes on what's mine. I tried to stop you before it came to this, but here we are. I should have put your ass in prison with some pictures implanted on your laptop."

"Nothing will keep me from her. Don't you realize that? Even if you send me to prison, they can't keep me forever. They never do. I'll just find her once I get out."

"Then I'll fucking kill you."

Del sits up and climbs off Sam. He throws me a look, but it's hard to see beneath the blood draining from his face. Behind him, Sam goes for a metal-handled broom sitting in the corner. Del looks around, his eyes furiously scanning for something that can be used as a weapon. He grabs a utility knife half-buried beneath a stack of pictures.

They clash again. The blade of the knife slips along the handle of the broom, sending sparks shooting. Arms and legs flail as they fight. Finally, there's a squelching sound, and I think the battle is over. That Del won.

But Del falls backward with the knife in his lower abdomen.

"No!" I scream, rattling the chair as I strain forward.

Del looks at me before falling to his knees. His hands clutch the blade as he stares at it with a look of disbelief. Sam struts over to taunt him.

"How does that feel? Not the lucky one now, huh?"

"Fuck you," Del hisses.

Sam pushes him, and Del falls onto his back. I'm almost certain I know what Sam plans to do now, and I can't watch Del die. The man I've come to care for. The man who accepted my fantasies and made them a reality.

I slam my eyes shut.

More squelching sounds come from the space in front of me. My stomach recoils and I gag. I'm listening to Del's murder.

I open my eyes.

Blood pours from Del's abdomen, but I don't see any other wounds. Then I see Sam. He's bent over, stumbling around with the knife lodged in his chest. Del must have pulled the knife from his gut and taken the opportunity to stab Sam while he was gloating.

His hand goes over his abdomen, and he holds pressure on the gushing wound as best he can. Sam falls forward and lies still, but the threat hasn't passed. If Del bleeds out, this was all for nothing.

I have to get to Del.

I use all the strength I can to rip one of the restraints off my arms. The skin feels like it's ripping from my bones, and I scream out as I break free. I don't care how much it hurts. I have to save him. Once one arm is free, I lean over and undo the other before unfastening my legs. Now that I'm completely free, I rip off my shirt and hold it to his wound. He smiles at me.

"Venti," he whispers. He's lost all the color in his face, and his clammy skin only assures me that we don't have a lot of time left together.

"You aren't allowed to die on me," I say as the blood spreads around my shirt and soaks my hands.

He licks his lips. "If I live, will you marry me?"

"*When* you live, I'll marry you. I promise."

Del inhales deeply, and I worry he's taken his last breath in front of me.

But it can't be his final breath. It can't.

Epilogue
One Year Later

Mariah

I shift my weight from one leg to the other. I'm so nervous to see what's outside of my blindfold. Del became such an important thing in my life. My hero. That night in the photo lab was a changing point for me, and now I'm back at a photo shoot again. After everything that happened, I'm back at the start of it all with a blindfold on. This time is a little different, though. I'm ready to see the person behind me.

"Are you ready to meet your blind date?" the photographer says.

It's a different woman this time, but she's just as excited about this. I couldn't face Sarah, knowing her brother is dead because of me. Well, he's dead because of himself, but she won't see it that way.

Tears fill my eyes as I nod my head. It's funny how things turn full circle.

"Take three steps forward, then turn around," she says.

I do as I'm told and take three heavy steps forward

before turning toward the other person. My stomach twists in knots at the thought of doing this again.

"Now take off your blindfolds."

I reach back and untie my blindfold with a hauntingly familiar motion. I let the strip of silk drop from my face, and the camera clicks beside me. A smile crosses my features as the man in front of me pulls off his blindfold. His tousled hair falls back into place, and a smile races to his face.

"Come here, venti," Del says, and I run for him. I leap into his arms and wrap my legs around his waist. There's a scar right about where I'm wrapped around him—a reminder of his willingness to protect me, even if it could cost him his life. It didn't that day, and I'm so grateful.

The camera flashes beside us as we relive the day we met.

Del sets me on my feet and drops to his knee. He pulls a box from his pocket and opens it in front of me. "This day last year, I nearly died, but a promise you made kept me going. Mariah Ree, will you honor that promise and marry me?"

Tears swell over my lids and drip down my cheeks at his reminder of this exact day, when I held his life in my hand beneath my bloody shirt. When I thought for sure he was dead, and the ambulance felt like it took forever to come. I remember sitting in the ER and waiting to hear that they'd done all they could, but he didn't make it. But that never happened. Finally they told me he was in critical condition but alive. We've been inseparable ever since.

"Yes! One hundred percent, yes!" I kiss him and the camera goes off beside our heads.

"I promise to always chase you when you want to run, venti, but I need you to promise me one more thing."

"Anything."

"Promise you'll start drawing again. I want to cover this scar with something beautiful."

I pull him into me and hug him. "I promise."

"I need a break," Del says, clutching his abdomen. I know he's not hurting. He just wants the photographer to leave.

"We can take fifteen," the photographer says. "I could use a smoke anyway." She walks toward the parking lot.

Del's eyes glance around the park's fall landscape. The trees are painted in their orange and yellow hues, with red splashed throughout.

"You should probably start running," he says.

My heart thumps in my chest, but it's not from fear this time. The excitement heats me up inside, and I take off toward the tree line, not too far from where we abandoned our blindfolds.

"If I catch you, prepare for a nightmare," he yells behind him.

I feel him closing the distance as I run. His footsteps beat in time with my heart. My breaths catch in my throat as his arms wrap around me. This time, I know for sure they're his arms. We crash to the soft ground, muddying our clothes. They'll be pissed at us when we get back to the shoot, but I don't care. I want to live in this moment.

Del's hands ride up my dirty thighs and spread my legs around him. He pulls my panties aside as he frees his cock and pushes inside me. He's maskless, and I'm glad because it means I can kiss him. Instead of pretending I don't want it, I make sure he knows just how much I do.

He rolls up his sleeves before pinning my arms. A new tattoo colors his skin. A tattoo of a knife through a heart with a little purple flower growing from the cut. I drew this one for him, and my heart swells with pride each time I see it.

His hips press me into the soft ground, and his lips spread on mine as he claims my mouth. Our hearts thunder against each other through our chests.

"Del," I pant.

He releases one of my hands and goes for my earlobe. He caresses it, and I moan against his mouth. He knows just how to touch me. Especially now that he can be himself. His hand leaves my ear and slips between us, where he rubs me until I'm bucking against him and staining the front of his black slacks with my wetness.

"I'm going to come, venti, but you can't clean up once I do. You have to finish this shoot as it drips between your legs. Can you do that?"

I nod my head, and we come in unison. The synchronization makes a feral groan leave his lips and land in my mouth. Coming together like that makes us feel like one body. One entity. As if each breath comes off the coattails of the other's.

"I love you," Del whispers against my mouth.

"I love you too," I pant.

Del and I met very unconventionally and fell for each other in an even more unconventional way. Now I only have one stalker.

And I wouldn't have it any other way.

If you want more novellas, check out these stories! Just keep in mind that most are much darker than this one:

Stranger Session

Wanted: Books2read.com/wantednovella
Her Fantasy: Books2read.com/HerFantasy
Toxic Love: Books2read.com/Toxic-Love

Make sure you check out my very dark, hitchhiker romance standalones as well:

Hitched: Books2read.com/Hitched
Along for the Ride: Books2read.com/MFMHitchhiker
Driving my Obsession: Books2read.com/
DrivingmyObsession

Connect with Lauren

Don't miss a thing from Lauren Biel! Check out all of her books, social media connections, and other important information at Campsite.bio/LaurenBielAuthor and Lauren Biel.com

Acknowledgments

Thank you to all my readers for your continued support. I wouldn't be where I am without you!

To my VIP gals (Lori, Kimberly, Jessie, Nikita, Lexi, Grace), I love you so much!

A big, huge thank you to my husband, who continues to support my author journey.

Thank you to my editor, Brooke, for making this novella shine.

Thank you to my valued Patrons. Your contributions helped make this book happen!

Lori, Jessie, Michelle M, Tabitha F, Lindsey S, Erika M, Laura T, Kayla W, Jennifer S, Nicole M, Eugenia M, Nineette W, Kimberly B, BoneDaddyAshe, Diana W, Ashley T, Kimberly S, Sammie Rae, Sarah, Allison B, Andrea J, Chelle, Gabby S, Hollie P, Jennifer H, Jessica G, Juli D, Samantha R, Sara S, XynideSuicide, @bethbetweenthepages, Sharee S, Samantha W, Lourdes G, Kelli T, Victoria R, Shelby F, Lauren P, Mackenzie H, Tiannah B, Wombles, Kristiana B, Vero A, Kayla H, Berthie, Deani, Amanda C, Brooke O, Kyla, Liza M, Ashley P, Mandy, Maddy, Cynthia B, Courtney P

Also by Lauren Biel

To view Lauren Biel's complete list of books, visit: https://laurenbiel.com/laurenbielbooks/

About the Author

Lauren Biel is the author of many dark romance books with several more titles in the works. When she's not working, she's writing. When she's not writing, she's spending time with her husband, her friends, or her pets. You might also find her on a horseback trail ride or sitting beside a waterfall in Upstate New York. When reading her work, expect the unexpected. To be the first to know about her upcoming titles, please visit www.LaurenBiel.com.

www.ingramcontent.com/pod-product-compliance
Lightning Source LLC
Chambersburg PA
CBHW061546310726
48972CB00008B/2640